HON

Viking Lore 1

Stormy Glenn

**EROTIC ROMANCE
MANLOVE**

Siren Publishing, Inc.
www.SirenPublishing.com

A SIREN PUBLISHING BOOK
IMPRINT: Erotic Romance ManLove

HONOR BOUND
Copyright © 2011 by Stormy Glenn

ISBN-10: 1-61034-877-X
ISBN-13: 978-1-61034-877-5

First Printing: August 2011

Cover design by Jinger Heaston
All cover art and logo copyright © 2011 by Siren Publishing, Inc.

ALL RIGHTS RESERVED: This literary work may not be reproduced or transmitted in any form or by any means, including electronic or photographic reproduction, in whole or in part, without express written permission.

All characters and events in this book are fictitious. Any resemblance to actual persons living or dead is strictly coincidental.

Printed in the U.S.A.

PUBLISHER
Siren Publishing, Inc.
www.SirenPublishing.com

DEDICATION

Kelley Sue, thanks for the wonderful title idea!

NOTE FROM STORMY

I love Norse mythology and all the possibilities that can be. However, please be aware that I have taken great liberty with the mythology of the Norse gods and Vikings to create my world. Of course, there's nothing out there that says this isn't the way things really could have happened…

HONOR BOUND

Viking Lore 1

STORMY GLENN
Copyright © 2011

Chapter 1

"I demand reparation! I demand a *weregild*!" Radulfr clenched his fists to hold back his fury as he gazed at those assembled.

"You are within your rights to demand a *weregild*, Jarl Radulfr," one of the lawspeakers said. "Do you have an amount in mind?"

Radulfr wanted to roll his eyes at the lawspeaker, but he knew it would do him no good. There was no amount of blood money that could be paid for the damage done to his people when they were attacked for no reason. Several of his people had been killed during the raid, many more were wounded. That didn't even begin to cover the loss of trade goods and livestock.

"Fafnir attacked my clan without provocation." Radulfr glared across the way to the dark-haired man that stood between two of the assembly's guards. "There are not enough silver coins made by the gods to compensate for the loss of life or livestock to my clan. I demand his life."

"A blood feud?" the lawspeaker gasped.

"A *holmgang*."

A woman cried out in the crowd, the sound suddenly cut off as quickly as it had been heard. He knew demanding a duel was almost unheard of in cases like this, but he wanted to get his hands on the man that had orchestrated the attack on his people. Fafnir's warriors had simply been following a command. Fafnir planned the attack and led the battle. He deserved to die for his crimes.

"Jarl Radulfr, you understand that Fafnir is the only living heir to this clan, the only son of their jarl. If you defeat him in battle, there will be no one to lead this clan after Jarl Dagr rests with the gods."

"I understand." Radulfr crossed his arms over his chest and continued to glare at Fafnir. "He should have thought of that before he attacked my clan. His territory borders mine, but we have lived in relative harmony for many years, long before I succeeded my *faðir* as jarl. His position will not keep him from paying for his crimes."

"Would Fafnir becoming a *warg* be sufficient?"

"No." Radulfr shook his head. "Banishing Fafnir for his crimes will only remove him from society. It will not make him pay for his crimes. I want his life."

"Radulfr, if Fafnir becomes a *warg*, he will be an outcast even from his own clan. He will no longer be considered human. Surely that is enough?"

Radulfr motioned with his hand to the warriors standing behind him. They rushed forward, pushing a small wagon in front of them until it came into view of all of those assembled. Radulfr heard the sudden inhales and gasps as the crowd saw the bodies piled inside the wagon, both human and livestock.

"Do you really believe that becoming a *warg* is enough compensation for what Fafnir has done? Would you like to ask the family members of those left behind?" Radulfr reached into the wagon and lifted out the body of a small child. "Why do you not ask this boy's mother how she feels about it? This, too, was her only son."

Radulfr held the child for a moment more then carefully laid him down in the wagon. He nodded to his men then watched them pull the wagon away, leaving only two of Radulfr's warriors with him. The soft sounds of crying followed the wagon as it was taken back to their territory.

"I demand a *holmgang*."

"Jarl Radulfr, Fafnir cannot hope to defeat you in a duel," the lawspeaker said. "He has not your strength."

"I know."

Radulfr grinned for the first time since the battle began a couple of days previous. He had no idea how Fafnir had been chosen as the next to succeed his faðir as jarl. The man had no code of honor, attacking women and children, raiding and pillaging for his own greed. He was not fit to rule.

"It is your right to demand a *holmgang*," the lawspeaker finally said. "Depriving a clan of their leadership has grave consequences for all. I wish you would reconsider. "

"I will not."

"Very well, a *holmgang* is ord—"

"Wait!"

Radulfr snapped around to see an older man running to the head of the crowd. His eyes narrowed when he spotted the gold thread embroidered on the hem of the man's tunic. He knew this man was somehow involved with Fafnir.

"Please, he is my only son, my only child," the man said. "I beg you not to take him from me."

Radulfr growled. It demeaned a jarl to beg. Fafnir was not a fit man for anything. His *faðir* should not be begging for his life. As jarl, he knew the rules of law as well as anyone, maybe even more.

"Please, as one jarl to another, I beg you not to take my only child from me. I know Fafnir is not a good man, but he is all I have."

"He is *huglausi*, cowardly," Radulfr spit out. "He does not deserve to live."

"A peace-pledge," the man said hurriedly, "would you consider a peace-pledge between our clans?"

Radulfr frowned. "I thought you said Fafnir was your only child?"

"There is another, not of my blood but of Fafnir's mother's."

"I have not heard of this child."

As far as Radulfr knew, Fafnir was Jarl Dagr's only offspring. Their clans bordered each other. They often traded together. They had even fought side by side in the past. There had never been mention of another.

"Ein has been raised these last two decades, since birth, away from our clan due to the circumstances surrounding his conception and my wife's infidelity." The Jarl's face flushed. "I am sure you understand."

The idea of a peace-pledge intrigued Radulfr simply because he did not currently have a wife of his own. Beyond satisfying his baser needs, he had yet to find anyone that aroused him enough to negotiate a marriage contract. There was also the added benefit of an alliance between their two clans. It would guarantee the reconciliation between the clans by marriage.

"And the bride price?" There was always a bride price to be paid for negotiating a marriage contract, the *mundr* and *morgengifu* were the responsibility of the groom and paid to the family of the bride. The dowry, or *heiman fylgia*, was paid by the bride's family to the husband.

"The *mundr* and *morgengifu* will of course be waved considering the situation," Jarl Dagr stated. "I will provide a *heiman fylgia* worth twice the *weregild* price of a jarl's *sonr*."

Radulfr barely kept his mouth from dropping open in astonishment. The *weregild* price for the son of a jarl could keep his clan in silver coin through several winters. Twice that amount would keep his clan in good health for years to come. It wouldn't compensate his clan members for the loss of their family members, but it would benefit the entire clan.

"We are at the beginning of the winter season," Radulfr said as another thought came to him. "If I agree to a peace-pledge between our clans, I will not wait until winter passes before claiming what is mine."

"No, of course not, I would not expect you to." The Jarl fidgeted for a moment, his fingers gripping the edges of his fur-lined cloak. "I believe we can forgo the normal wedding rituals and complete the *hansal* right here."

"Jarl Dagr is correct, Jarl Radulfr," the lawspeaker said as he waved his hands around to indicate those assembled. "We have enough people here to witness the *handsal*. We simply need your agreement to make the marriage negotiations complete and you can retrieve your bride."

"I would speak with my men first."

The lawspeaker nodded. Radulfr turned and walked the few feet to the two men standing behind him. He could see the looks of disbelief on the faces of the two men he trusted more than any other, Vidarr and Haakon, his best friends and confidants.

"Your thoughts?"

"Do you really want to align yourself or our clan with Fafnir's after what he did?" Haakon asked. "The man needs to be taught a lesson. This seems too much like he is being given a free ride."

"I agree, but the bride price would well-compensate our clan and keep us in good health for many winters to come."

"But a *hansal*, Radulfr?" Haakon asked. "That's a formal agreement of betrothal sealed by a hand-clasp. By your honor, it cannot be taken back once you shake Jarl Dagr's hand. You will be bound to take this bride as your own no matter how ugly she is."

"She could be a beauty," Radulfr said.

"And be related to Fafnir?" Haakon smirked. "I don't think so."

Radulfr rolled his eyes and turned his attention to Vidarr. "You haven't said anything."

"I do not believe there is anything to say. Harm was done to our clan. Life and property were lost. Yes, there would be great satisfaction in the taking of Fafnir's life, of seeing his blood coat our weapons. However, that satisfaction would be short-lived."

"In other words, you think I should agree to the peace-pledge?"

"While it would not give us the same pleasure as taking the man's life, a peace-pledge between our clans would align us. An attack on us by anyone else would be an attack on them. The bride price alone leans me in that direction."

Vadirr looked thoughtful for a moment, his eyebrows drawing together. Radulfr waited. Vadirr was a thinker, and Radulfr knew he would have to wait until the man was ready to talk before he heard a word come out of his mouth.

"The crops, livestock, and our recent trade missions have done us well this year. We are not hurting for either coin or resources to care for our own. However, the *weregild* of twice that of a jarl's *sonr* would ensure that our clan had many winters of good health and food. The worry for our clan would be less."

"But is it enough to ease the grief of our clan members who lost family members?" Radulfr asked.

"Will taking Fafnir's life bring more than a momentary satisfaction?" Vidarr countered. "Or would the knowledge that Fafnir is paying for years to come make our clan members feel better?"

"You mean his *faðir* is paying."

"I actually believe you can stipulate that the *weregild* come from Fafnir, can't you?" Vadirr asked.

Radulfr pressed his lips together as a smile threatened to break out. Now would not be the time to show his enjoyment of the idea of Fafnir paying through the nose for what he had done. Not only would Radulfr have a bride and an alliance with another clan, which was always a good thing, but he could demand that Fafnir be the one to pay the bride price.

"Very well." Radulfr turned back to the assembly. He drew in a deep breath before addressing the lawspeaker. "I agree to the peace-pledge. However, Fafnir will be paying the bride price as stated, not his *faðir*."

"What?" Fafnir shouted, lunging forward. "You can't do that."

"Can't I?"

"Jarl Radulfr is within his rights to demand you pay the bride price, Fafnir," the lawspeaker said. "You did plan and lead the attack on his clan. Since a bride price has been agreed upon and suggested by your *faðir* and jarl, you will be responsible for paying it."

"But I don't have that kind of coin."

"Maybe you should have thought of that before you attacked another clan," the lawspeaker said. He turned to look at Radulfr. "As jarl, do you agree to the terms set forth in these negotiations?"

"I do," Radulfr replied, knowing full well that once he spoke the words of the agreement over a handclasp with Jarl Dagr that they could not be taken back. To do so would bring shame upon him and his clan, a fate worse than death in Radulfr's mind.

The lawspeaker turned to look at Fafnir's *faðir*. "As jarl, do you agree to the terms set forth in these negotiations?"

"I do."

"Please select two of your warriors to witness the *hansal*," the lawmaker said. "I will add two of the *Thingstead*'s warriors as well so that no one clan can claim undue pressure or influence."

Radulfr waved Vidarr and Haakon forward. He watched the other jarl and lawspeaker wave two of their guards forward. When all six men were assembled, Radulfr stepped forward and clasped his hand to the jarl's.

"I bond myself in lawful betrothal to Ein, and with this handclasp, I agree to fulfill and observe the whole agreement between us, which has been said in the hearing of these six witnesses without duplicity or cunning."

The jarl nodded at Radulfr's words. "As jarl and *fastnandi*, the guardian responsible for Ein's interests during these negotiations, with this handclasp I agree to fulfill and observe the whole agreement between us, which has been said in the hearing of these six witnesses without duplicity or cunning."

"As these formal words of hansal have been observed, so shall they be," the lawspeaker said. "Fafnir, you have one fortnight to turn over the bride price to Jarl Radulfr as agreed upon here."

Radulfr slowly let out the breath he had been holding. That was it. He was officially betrothed to Ein. The only thing that remained of the ceremony to make it complete was the exchange of rings between them and the observance by the witnesses that the wedding had been consummated.

Radulfr wasn't looking forward to having onlookers while he claimed his bride, but it was tradition. In formal agreements such as this and due to the fact that most people who married did so for economical reasons or in cases like this, a peace-pledge, witnesses were required to ensure that the wedding had been consummated. This was not a love match.

"Now, where is my bride?"

Chapter 2

"Ein."

Startled at the sudden words, Ein swung around to see a rather shabbily dressed man standing several feet from his position. He thought he was alone out in the gardens. "*Grandfaðir?*"

The old man smiled and gestured with his hand for Ein to come closer. "Come, I wish to speak with you."

Ein climbed to his feet and brushed his hands off before hurrying over to his *grandfaðir*. It wasn't often he received a visit from the man, and he was eager to spend time with him. The *godis*, or temple-priests of the *hov*, the spiritual commune where Ein lived, might be kindly men, but they were not his *grandfaðir*.

"How have you been, Ein?" his *grandfaðir* asked as they walked. "Have the *godis* been treating you well?"

"Things are well enough, *Grandfaðir*." Ein gestured back to the garden he had been working in when his *grandfaðir* arrived. "I've been working in the garden a lot, and I like that. I seem to have an affinity for growing things."

"Your *faðir* is the god of fertility." Njörðr chuckled. "Did you expect anything less?"

"How is my *faðir?*" Ein hated to ask, but he hadn't seen his *faðir* in over three winters. He missed him. But it wasn't often that his *faðir* could get away from the watchful eye of his wife, Gerðr.

She was known as a very jealous woman and hated the fact that Freyr had created a child with another woman, a human woman at that. Ein had felt her wrath on more than one occasion, usually when he got into trouble not of his own making.

"Your *faðir* is well, *Grandsonr*. Forever trying to escape his wife's clutches." Njörðr clasped his hands behind his back and looked out over the landscape. He seemed to be gathering his thoughts as if what he had to say would be profound.

"*Grandfaðir*, is something wrong?"

"I have come to discuss a grave matter with you, Ein."

"Grave?" Ein swallowed past the lump that suddenly formed in his throat. "What do you mean grave?"

"Men will soon arrive to take you from this place."

"What?" Ein started to panic, looking quickly around as if he could see the raiders coming. "Why?"

"You have been betrothed by Jarl Dagr."

Ein's mouth dropped open as he stopped walking to stare at his *grandfaðir*. "Can he do that? He's not my real *faðir*."

"Technically, that is true and you could bring protest before the Thing assembly. However, I do not believe that would be in your best interest." Njörðr waved his hand around the small spiritual commune where Ein lived almost all of his life. "This is not the place for you, Ein. You were meant for better things."

"But I like it here, *Grandfaðir*," Ein protested, the thought of leaving the only home he had ever known making his heart ache. "They're nice to me here. They let me work in the garden and everything."

"The path before you will not be an easy one, *grandsonr*, but it will be a rewarding one in the end."

Ein glanced down at the ground as he walked beside his *grandfaðir*. The thought of leaving the *hov* scared him a lot. Since the day he'd been brought to the commune just after his birth, he had never set foot outside of the gates surrounding it. He had no desire to do so now.

"Do I really have to go, *Grandfaðir*?"

"No, you can stay here if that is your wish, but I urge you to consider your options first. You will never find a mate or have a family if you stay here. You will not get to experience the world around us here inside this commune."

"A mate?" Ein scoffed then felt his face heat as he flushed. "*Grandfaðir*, I don't... um..."

"I am fully aware of your preferences, Ein." Njörðr chuckled. "Your betrothed is Jarl Radulfr. He is a good man, governing a large clan in the northern regions. I would not have allowed you to be betrothed to a man I did not approve of."

"I'm betrothed to a man?"

Ein was shocked. He had never heard of such a thing. Sure, people heard of men being together sexually. It happened quite often, especially during times of war when women were scarce. He'd just never heard of two men being betrothed.

"Is that even legal?"

"The agreement has been made, Ein, the *handsal* witnessed by six witnesses and a lawspeaker. To break the agreement would bring shame on all parties involved."

"Like Jarl Dagr cares about bringing shame on anyone," Ein scoffed. "This is the same man that beat my *móðir* to death after she gave birth to me, remember?"

"And that will always be regretted by your *faðir* and myself." Njörðr grimaced as he faced Ein. "If we had acted in time, your *móðir* would still be alive today. Her death rests fully on our shoulders."

"Don't fool yourself, *Grandfaðir*. My *móðir*'s death rests on the shoulders of Jarl Dagr. He's the one that killed her because of me."

"Jarl Dagr knew your *móðir* was a favorite of the gods. He knew she had been chosen to give birth to you. Although, I suspect that is the only reason you are alive. He could have killed you like he did your *móðir*. I will be forever grateful that he brought you here instead."

"He's afraid of you."

"And rightly so." Njörðr chuckled.

"I still don't understand why you allowed him to agree to a betrothal for me."

"It was not for his benefit, believe me."

"You can't tell me it was for mine."

"Jarl Radulfr will take good care of you once he gets over his initial shock."

Ein skidded to a stop once again, staring in shock at his *grandfaðir*. "He doesn't know I'm a man?"

"No. Jarl Radulfr only knows that he has been betrothed to someone named Ein. He will discover who you are when he arrives."

Ein could feel his face pale as coldness filled him. "Do–does he know I am only half human?"

"No, and you are not to tell him. Jarl Radulfr must not know of your connection to your *faðir* or the *álfar*."

"But I'm half *álfar*. How can I hide being part Elvin from him?" Ein flipped his braid behind his back and brushed the hair back from his ears. "How am I supposed to hide these?" he asked as he pointed to his sharply pointed ears.

"Ein, I told you that this path will not be an easy one, but as long as you do as I say, the rewards you will receive will be great."

Ein groaned as he rubbed his hands down his face. His *grandfaðir's* grand plan was going to get him killed. "What if he has questions? I shouldn't hide things from someone I'm supposed to spend the rest of my life with."

"All of his questions will be answered in good time, Ein."

"You mean he will find out who I am in time?" Ein asked as he let his hands fall back to his side. "How? I thought I wasn't to tell him."

"That is not for me to say right now, but all will be revealed to you and Radulfr in time. Just do as I have said until I say otherwise."

"Well, that isn't cryptic, is it?"

Njörðr chuckled again. "I suppose it is, but it is all I can give you at this point."

Ein sighed and look out over the fields of grain growing, the cattle, and other livestock milling about. He lived a simple life here at the *hov*. He worked in the garden and fields, helped tend the livestock, and meditated with the others in the commune. He wasn't sure he was ready for anything more.

"I'm scared, *Grandfaðir*."

"I know, Ein, and you have reason to be. Things will not be easy for you for a while. The *hansal* came about by way of a peace-pledge."

Ein inhaled sharply. He clenched his hands together to keep them from trembling. "A peace-pledge?" he whispered.

Njörðr nodded. "Your half brother, Fafnir attacked Jarl Radulfr's clan, killing several and injuring many more. While a *handsal* has taken place, there will be animosity toward you by those of Radulfr's clan until they get to know you. You must be prepared for that."

"They're going to hate me."

"There will be those that will not hold you in a good light, but there will be even more that will come to care for you a great deal, Ein, especially Radulfr. He needs someone like you to stand by his side as he rises to power. Radulfr has been chosen by the gods for great things, just as you have, my boy. You just need to hold out until that happens."

"How do you know all of this?"

"I am a god, Ein. There is not much I do not know."

Ein nodded. Yes, his *grandfaðir* was a god, associated with sea, seafaring, wind, fishing, wealth, and crop fertility. He just wished that sometimes the man would be less of a god and more of a *grandfaðir*. Things were never simple when dealing with the gods, though.

"What do I do now?"

"Your betrothed will be here by nightfall. That should give you the time you need to pack and be prepared for his arrival. After you have packed, you need to follow the ritual marriage preparations." Njörðr reached into his cloak and pulled out two small vials, one silver and one gold. "Pour the silver one into your bath water. Drink the gold one once you're in your bath."

Ein took the vials and looked at them. They were solid, giving no clue to what they contained inside but the runes etched on the outside of each vial were intricate, even if Ein couldn't read the runes. "What are they?"

"Presents from your *faðir*."

Ein frowned. Somehow, with the knowledge that his *faðir* had sent the two vials, Ein knew whatever they contained would change his life. He just wasn't sure in what way. His *faðir* was cousin to Loki, the god of mischief. Freyr could be very imaginative.

"You better get going, Ein. Your time is running short."

Ein glanced around, noting that the sun was starting to fall. If his *grandfaðir* was correct and Jarl Radulfr would arrive by nighttime, then he needed to get going. He didn't have much to pack, but the wedding preparations could take some time, especially since he had no one to help him prepare.

"Thank you, *Grandfaðir*."

"I'm sure at this moment you don't really mean that, Ein, but you will in time. Just remember to use the vials as I directed."

"Yes, *Grandfaðir*."

Ein watched as his *grandfaðir* walked off, disappearing in a glint of sunlight. He quickly glanced around to see if anyone else had seen his *grandfaðir* disappear, but no one was paying either of them any attention. Ein chuckled.

Njörðr always appeared to Ein dressed in shabby clothing so he didn't draw undue attention. Anyone looking would have thought that Ein was just talking to another field worker. They would have no clue the man was a god.

He clutched the vials to his chest and walked back toward the *byre* where his room was located. Not being a *godi*, Ein wasn't housed with the others in the commune. He had a small room at one end of the *byre* where the animals were kept. But it was all his own. He didn't have to sleep in the communal *langhus* with everyone else. He had privacy, and he was going to need it if he had to prepare for his betrothed.

"Ein, where do you head? Darkness has not yet fallen."

Ein glanced over to see one of the *godi* looking at him. He smiled and quickly pushed the vials into his tan tunic. Only the head priest knew Ein was the *sonr* of a god. The others believed he was simply an orphan. He wasn't allowed to tell them otherwise.

"I was heading to talk with *Godi* Asmundr." That was a plausible excuse. Besides, he should probably inform the head *godi* that he would be leaving and that they were expecting guests.

"Well, be quick about it then. We still have good daylight left."

Ein nodded and hurried on his way. The quicker he explained things to *Godi* Asmundr, the quicker he could pack and get ready. Ein went to the main longhouse and stepped inside. He looked around, spotting *Godi* Asmundr sitting by the hearth.

"*Godi* Asmundr, can I have a moment of your time?" Ein asked when he reached the man.

"Ein," the man said as he stood up, "you look upset, *sonr*, what seems to be the problem?"

Ein glanced around at the other people sitting by the hearth. Some pretended to be preoccupied by what they were doing, but Ein knew they listened avidly. Still others blatantly watched. Gossip was rampant in a small commune like this one.

"I need to speak with you privately, *Godi* Asmundr," he said as he looked back at the *godi*. "It's really important."

Godi Asmundr arched an eyebrow for a moment then nodded. "Very well, Ein, I can give you a few minutes, but you'd better be quick. I have meditation soon."

"Yes, *Godi* Asmundr, I will be very quick." Ein turned and hurried out of the *langhus*, walking several feet away from the building. The walls were thin, and anything could be heard through them. Ein didn't need eavesdroppers.

Ein bounced nervously from foot to foot as he waited for the *godi* to join him. His heart was thundering in his chest. Ein didn't know if it came from the impending arrival of Jarl Radulfr or the talk he needed to have with *Godi* Asmundr. He just knew he was nervous.

"What is this all about, Ein?" *Godi* Asmundr asked. "What is so important that you had to pull me away from my students?"

"I had a visitor earlier."

"A visitor?"

"Njörðr ."

Godi Asmundr's eyebrows shot up. "Your *grandfaðir* came to see you?"

Ein nodded. "He brought news."

"What sort of news?"

"I've been betrothed to Jarl Radulfr. He should be arriving by nightfall."

"You've been betrothed?"

Ein nodded.

"To a man?"

"That's what I said, but my *grandfaðir* assured me that this was how things were supposed to happen." Ein shrugged. "I don't really understand it, but I wasn't about to argue with my *grandfaðir*. He also said my *faðir* approved it."

"Well, I suppose that changes things a bit then, doesn't it?" The man rubbed his hand down his long white beard. "I guess we should get you ready then."

"I know the basics of what I need to do, and I was going to do it, but I thought you might want to be informed that we had guests coming first."

"Yes, yes, that is true. We need to prepare for visitors. Did your *grandfaðir* tell you how many men would be arriving?"

"No, he just said I needed to be ready by nightfall."

"Very well." *Godi* Asmundr waved his hand off toward the *byre*. "Go get ready. I'll make sure the bathhouse is made available to you and inform the others of our guests. You just worry about being prepared to meet your betrothed. I'll see to the wedding feast."

"Oh, I don't—"

"Ein, you have been a child of this *hov* since you were a wee babe. We will not send you out into the world without a proper send-off."

"There's something more, *Godi* Asmundr." Ein twisted his hands together nervously.

"More?"

"Jarl Radulfr doesn't know who I am, and my *grandfaðir* says he's not to know. Not right now. He also doesn't know I'm a man."

"He believes he is coming to claim a female?"

Ein swallowed hard and nodded. "Yes."

"This may not go well for you, Ein. There is no telling of this man's temper once he learns he has been deceived. I am concerned for your welfare."

"My *grandfaðir* assured me that Jarl Radulfr is a man of honor. I have to believe he knows what he is talking about." Ein prayed his *grandfaðir* was right. He didn't want to be on the receiving end of anyone's anger.

"Well, you'd better go get ready, Ein. You haven't much time before nightfall."

"Thank you, *Godi* Asmundr." Ein turned to go.

"Ein, I will be sad to see you go. You have been a great asset to this *hov*. I hope you know you will be missed."

Ein turned back, his eyes misting as he gazed upon the man that had acted as substitute *faðir* for him his entire life. "I won't be gone forever. I'll come and visit if I can."

The *godi* smiled and clasped his hands together in front of him. "You will still be missed, Ein."

Ein nodded, too choked up to reply. He turned and hurried off to his room before he broke down and started crying. Despite the long hours of labor in the fields, the knowledge that he would never truly belong here, Ein would still miss the people. He'd spent his entire life here. He didn't really wish to leave, but it seemed the decision had been taken out of his hands.

Ein blinked several times and swallowed past the lump building in his throat as he reached his room. He didn't have much to pack as the *hov* disdained personal items. He was only allowed them because he wasn't in training to be a future *godi* to the gods.

It took Ein less than ten minutes to pack all of his belongings into one small satchel. All of his worldly possessions consisted of a few changes of clothing, some wood carvings he'd made throughout the years, some rare seeds, and a heavy winter fur pelt.

Ein set his belongings by the door. He grabbed a fresh change of clothes and left his room, heading for the communal bathhouse. He just hoped the *Godi* Asmundr had cleared everyone out before he got there. Ein didn't like sharing the communal bathhouse with the others, preferring instead to bathe in private.

Luckily, the bathhouse was empty just as *Godi* Asmundr said it would be. Ein shut the door behind him and walked to the deep wooden barrel that they bathed in. It was only used for special occasions, but Ein supposed this would qualify.

He turned on the water spigot and watched as hot water from the natural hot springs under the bathhouse filled the tub. As it filled, Ein got undressed and folded his clothes, setting them on the bench near the door. He grabbed the two vials his *grandfaðir* had given him out of his tunic and carried them over to the water.

He held one in each hand, looking from one to the other. Did his *grandfaðir* say drink the gold one and pour the silver into his bathwater or drink the silver one and pour the gold one into his bathwater? Ein couldn't remember.

Ein shrugged and climbed into the tub, wincing as the hot water hit his naked body. He knew his *faðir* wouldn't give him anything that would harm him. He sat down and opened one vial, pouring the contents into the water. He opened the other vial and drank it down, grimacing as the sour taste slid down his throat. He felt his skin immediately started to tingle.

Maybe he had gotten them mixed up. He had no idea. He was so too worried about the impending arrival of Jarl Radulfr to concerned with which vial of liquid went where. He probably should be concerned, but he just wasn't, not right now. He could be worried about the vials later.

Ein grabbed some soap and began cleaning himself up from head to toe. The preparation rituals said that the bride and groom needed to be cleaned from head to toe, washing away their old life and preparing themselves for their new life.

Ein didn't understand it, but he was willing to do pretty much anything to have the hot water to himself. Washing down at the river near the commune wasn't much fun, but it was the only place he could be assured that he could wash in private.

Once he was clean, Ein climbed out of the tub and put on the clean clothes he had brought with him. He smoothed down the white tunic, hoping there were no stains. When he couldn't find any, Ein tucked his pants into the tops of his leather boots.

Lastly, he grabbed the two empty vials and tucked them back in his tunic. They were made of gold and silver. There was no telling if he was going to need some sort trading material in the future. He had no idea what the future might hold.

Ein pulled the plug on the tub, making sure that the water drained out then quickly cleaned it. He didn't know what he had poured into the tub, but he did know it was just meant for him.

Once the tub was clean, Ein grabbed his dirty clothes and left the bathhouse, heading back to his room. He could hear a rush of activity by the gate just as he reached the *byre* and knew his betrothed had arrived.

His heart pounded ferociously in his chest and his knees started to buckle as soon as he stepped inside of his room and shut the door. Ein quickly sat down on the wooden platform where he slept and dropped his head into his hands.

He couldn't believe that in just a few minutes he would meet the man he was destined to spend the rest of his life with. Jarl Radulfr would have complete control over him, especially considering that the man was the chieftain of his clan. As jarl, he had final decisions that pertained to his clan members within the bounds of the laws, even life or death.

At the sudden hard knock on his door, Ein sat up. He couldn't help but wonder if this would mean his death. He drew in a deep breath and clenched his hands at his sides as he tried to gather his courage.

"Come in."

Chapter 3

Radulfr knocked impatiently on the wooden door inside the *byre*. He didn't know what to think when he had asked for Ein and been directed to a building that housed the farm animals. He could think of no reason his bride would be inside of a *byre*.

"Come in."

Radulfr frowned as he opened the door and stepped inside. The voice he heard sounded suspiciously like a man's voice. If that was so, Radulfr wanted to know why a man was inside a closed room with his betrothed.

His eyes were immediately drawn to the small figure sitting on a raised platform sitting across the room from him. He was mesmerized by slightly paled skin hidden under streams of sunlight blond hair. It took all of his finely honed control to look away from the alluring form and around the rest of the room.

"I am looking for Ein," he said when he didn't see anyone else in the small room.

"I'm Ein."

Radulfr's eyes snapped back to the person sitting on the platform. He peered closer and knew he was definitely looking at a man, but he couldn't dismiss the stirring he felt in his groin at the vision before him. He just didn't understand it.

"You are Ein?" The man nodded, swallowing so hard that Radulfr could hear it from his position by the door. "*Sonr* of Jarl Dagr?"

"Jarl Dagr is not my *faðir*, but I am who you are looking for."

"I'm looking for a woman," Radulfr snapped.

"I'm sorry you were deceived, but as you can see," Ein stood up and held his hands out to his sides, "I am not a woman, and Jarl Dagr knows it well."

"By Thor's hammer," Radulfr whispered, "I've been bonded to a man."

Radulfr couldn't begin to describe the rage that instantly flooded him, but he could see it mirrored in Ein's fear as the man stepped back from him, eyeing him warily.

"I'm sorry you were deceived," Ein said again. "I'm sure under the circumstances that you can bring suit against Jarl Dagr before the lawspeakers and have the *hansal* nullified."

Radulfr's eyes narrowed as he heard Ein's words. "We rode through the night to reach this *hov*. No one could have gotten here before us. How did you even know about the *hansal*?"

If anything, Ein's face paled even more as he shrugged. "I just do."

"That answer is not good enough, Ein." Radulfr crossed his arms over his chest to keep himself from reaching for the man and giving him a good shake. "Was this whole thing set up by Dagr and Fafnir? Were you involved?"

"No, please, you have to believe me. Fafnir and I may have had the same mother, but I've never even met the man. I only know of Jarl Dagr because he pays a foster fee to the *hov* to house me. He doesn't want me returning to his land and bringing his shame to light before his clan. I swear I had nothing to do with any of this."

"Then tell me how you know we were betrothed."

"Someone stopped by and told me to expect you."

"Who?"

"Just some old man."

"And you believed him?" Radulfr snorted.

"You're here, aren't you?"

Radulfr gritted his teeth at Ein's sarcastic answer. He needed to maintain control of his emotions, especially his anger. Losing control could be dangerous for everyone, including Radulfr.

"Who was this old man?"

Ein pressed his lips together and shrugged. Radulfr narrowed his eyes. It was clear that he wasn't going to get any answers out of Ein. He just hoped the man didn't continue to fight him when they reached home, or things would go very badly for both of them. Radulfr didn't like being thwarted.

Radulfr stepped back and leaned again the wall, taking a deep breath as he suddenly realized he had already decided to take Ein home with him. He just didn't know if that decision came from his own sense of honor or the way the man looked.

He had to admit, as men went, Ein was by far one of the most attractive Radulfr had ever seen. His skin had a porcelain quality but seemed to almost shine in the soft light from the moon shining through the window.

Ein wasn't a big man, certainly not as big as Radulfr was. He'd never make a warrior. Radulfr couldn't say he was disappointed in the fact. He didn't like the idea of his betrothed being in battle. He'd much prefer to come home and have someone welcome him back.

The smoky silver eyes that kept peering over at him between strands of long white blond hair intrigued Radulfr more than anything. Ein's eyes were very expressive. Radulfr thought he might be able to see his soul mirrored in those smoky depths.

"I know why I agreed to the peace-pledge," Radulfr finally said after several moments of silence. "Why did you? It is your right to deny the *handsal*."

"The old man pointed out to me that I have spent nearly all of my life here at the *hov*. I am unlikely to meet anyone here that is marriageable. If I don't, I will never be able to go out into the world and experience what it has to offer."

Radulfr wasn't sure how he felt about that statement beyond the fact that it made him want to growl. "And how do you feel about being betrothed to me?"

Ein's face flushed, and he looked quickly down at the floor. "I'm okay with it. The old man assured me that you were an honorable man."

"I sure would like to meet this old man of yours."

Silver eyes flashed up at him. "Maybe you will someday."

He didn't know who this old man was that Ein kept talking about or how Ein knew him, but Radulfr had the distinct feeling he might be seeing him one day, too. And he would have a lot of questions for the old man when he did.

"How do you feel about this betrothal?"

"I don't know. I never really thought about one before today."

"Fair enough, but you do understand that this is for life, right? There are very few reasons for divorce in our world, and none that would pertain to either of us unless you plan on sleeping around on me."

Ein's face flushed again. "No."

"And as I will not raise a hand against you, then there should be no reason for us to bring any grievance before the assembly. If you agree to this *handsal*, and I will have your agreement before we consummate it, then we will not be separated except in death."

"I understand."

"Do you agree to the *hansal* and all that it entails?" Radulfr started to hold his breath in anticipation of Ein's reply. He barely caught himself in time, blowing out the air he almost held in.

"Can I ask you something first?"

"Yes."

"I know this is a peace-pledge. Even though I have never met him, nor do I wish to, I understand that Fafnir killed several members of your clan. How will they accept me after what my half brother did that?"

"However I tell them to." The blond eyebrow that Ein arched was almost amusing to Radulfr, as if the man was taking him to task. "People have been killed, that is true. And your half brother is responsible, but in the end, I think they will see this *hansal* as a benefit to our people. Jarl Dagr has agreed to pay twice the *weregild* of a jarl's *sonr* as your bride price while waving *mundr* and *morgengifu*."

"This is true?" Ein's eyes widened when Radulfr nodded. "I didn't even know he had that much money. He complains to *Godi* Asmundr every year when he brings my foster fee that he doesn't have the money to pay for my upkeep."

"The bride price will not come from Jarl Dagr but from his *sonr*, Fafnir. He's the one who planned the attack and led his solders against us. It is his debt to pay."

"And mine, apparently."

"You can refuse. I will not take you from this place if you do not wish to go." Radulfr would have a willing betrothed, man or woman, or he wouldn't have one at all. He faced a lot of discord in protecting his people. He didn't need it in his bedchamber.

"I have said I agree to the *handsal*, and I do."

"So you can leave this place?"

"My understanding is that this will be a good match, the two of us. You've shown honor in just the time you've been in this room. You could have turned and walked away the minute you saw that I was a man, but you didn't. I believe that bodes well for us."

"You do realize that it will not be easy being betrothed to me, do you not?" While he could see the merits of Ein's words, Radulfr still felt the need to warn the man. "I am jarl. As my betrothed, you will be *griomenn*, the homeman, taking over my household. There will be those that will not look favorably upon you for this choice."

"I understand that I am taking the lesser role, but certainly no one could expect me to do anything else. You are the stronger of the two of us. Your place is clearly that of the *husbondi*. No would ever mistake me for the master of the house."

Radulfr chuckled. He could see Ein's point. No one would ever see him as the master of the house. As fine as it was, Ein didn't have an intimidating bone in his body. Radulfr wasn't even sure the man could run a household. No one would listen to him unless he climbed on a table and jumped up and down.

"You do also realize that in order for the *hansal* to be completed, we need to exchange rings and have the consummation of the wedding night observed by witnesses."

Ein's face started to burn again but then suddenly paled. "People are going to watch us?"

"It is custom, Ein, for the wedding night to be observed by witnesses so that no one can say that it was not consummated. The same six men that witnessed the *handsal* with Jarl Dagr will stand witness for us tonight. They rode with me."

"But…" Ein's hands twisted together. "Have you ever done something like this?"

"Consummate a betrothal?" Radulfr asked. "No. I have, however, witnessed a few."

"No, I mean… you know…" Ein waved his hand between him and Radulfr. "Have you ever…"

"Been with a man?"

Ein's face turned beet red as he nodded and looked down at the floor again.

"I have been with a man a time or two. It is not that much different than being with a woman except that the equipment is just a bit different."

"I've not been with either. I wouldn't know."

"I'll be changing that before the sun rises in the morning."

Radulfr couldn't begin to understand that strong feeling of possessiveness he suddenly felt upon hearing of Ein's virginal status.

Knowing he would be the only one to ever have the man made him want to howl at the moon.

He all of a sudden felt needy and achy and on the edge of his control. Radulfr moved crossed the room and grabbed Ein's arms, pulling the man up tight against his body. He arched an eyebrow at the small inhale of breath that came from Ein.

"You do know how this is done, do you not?"

"So—sort of."

"Like this."

Radulfr curled one hand around the back of Ein's neck and wrapped the other around his waist, drawing the man even closer as he leaned down and claimed his lips. The small shudder of Ein's body when their tongues met was a welcome surprise. It seemed his betrothed was not immune to him.

Radulfr licked at Ein's lips, caressing them with his tongue before delving inside to swipe up the sweet taste that was uniquely Ein's. The man tasted wonderful, like the sweetest honeyed wine. Radulfr's groan was low, his head almost spinning like he had already drank the wine.

When air became a necessity and Ein began to slump against him, Radulfr reluctantly lifted his head and looked down into the dazed silver eyes staring back at him. "And that, my little *kisa*, is how that is done."

Ein's mouth opened and closed several times like a fish. He finally pressed them together for a moment then licked his lips. "Okay."

Radulfr chuckled and led Ein toward the door. "I need to introduce you to my men, Vadirr and Haakon, as well as the other witnesses who accompanied me to get you. The sooner we get this done, the sooner we can head home. The weather is going to start getting bad soon, and we need to go before that happens."

"Tell me about your home," Ein said. "What is it like?"

"It's colder than here, I can tell you that much." Radulfr chuckled as he remembered Haakon complaining about how warm the southern region was as they arrived in the area. "I hope you're prepared for a lot of cold wintery nights because we have more of them than anything else."

"How cold are we talking?"

Radulfr gestured to the thin cotton tunic and pants Ein wore. "These are fine for inside the longhouse or maybe summer clothes, but they would never cut it during the winter season. You'd freeze to death before you got fifty feet from the door."

"Just how long is the winter season?"

"From start to finish, about nine months, but that includes the months warming up for summer and cooling down for winter. The middle months are the harshest. We've been known to get snow above the windows before."

"Snow?" Ein's face lit up. "Real snow?"

Radulfr frowned and tilted his head slightly. "Is there any other kind?"

"I've just never seen real snow. We get lots of rain around here and even some frost, but we've never had snow before."

"Oh, then yes, it is definitely real snow." Radulfr chuckled as he thought about the long winters at home. "And lots of it. We spend a lot of time indoors during the winter, usually making things for the first spring trade."

"What about raising crops? Can you do that with such cold weather?"

"Yes, we do raise crops and livestock."

"What kind of crops?"

Radulfr arched an eyebrow as Ein started bouncing around beside him. The man was practically buzzing with excitement. "We raise several different types of crops depending on the field rotation and time of year—everything from barley to vegetables and fruit. Why?"

"I love working in the gardens. Do you think I'd be allowed to do that?"

"Work in the fields?" Radulfr couldn't think of a job he hated more, but if Ein liked it… "Yes, I suppose that would be okay."

"I'm really good at it." Ein seemed particularly proud of that fact, and Radulfr couldn't help but smile at the excitement he could see radiating from Ein's face.

"How are you with farm animals?"

"I do okay. I mean, I like them and all, but I'm better in the gardens."

"The gardens it is then."

Ein seemed pleased with that statement, and Radulfr couldn't help being pleased himself with Ein's reaction. He didn't have a lot of experience in relationships, but maybe it wouldn't be that hard. Ein seemed easily contented.

Radulfr pulled Ein to a stop when they reached the door of the *hov langhus*. "Are you sure you're okay with this? Leaving your home and all?" He wished he hadn't said anything when the happy little smile fell from Ein's lips.

"I'll miss this place and especially *Godi* Asmundr. They are all I've ever known. But I suppose everyone has to move on at some point."

"I don't know when we'll be able to come back to visit, but I promise we will."

The corners of Ein's lips started to turn up as his smile returned. "I'd really like that."

Radulfr smiled, trying to reassure Ein, then turned and led him into the *langhus*. He could feel several sets of eyes narrow in on him and Ein the moment they stepped inside. Radulfr tightened his grip on Ein's arm as he searched for Vidarr and Haakon.

Spotting them standing by the hearth in the middle of the room, he headed in that direction. He could see the surprise on his friends' faces as he approached and couldn't help but wonder how they would react when they discovered the sexy little man he held onto was his betrothed.

"Vadirr, Haakon," Radulfr said once they stopped in front of the two men, "I'd like you to meet Ein, my betrothed."

"But…" Haakon looked totally confused as he glanced between Radulfr and Ein. "He's a man."

"I'm fully aware of that." It was kind of hard to miss. Ein might have an ethereal beauty, but he still looked like a man—just not a warrior. "That does not change the fact that Ein is indeed my betrothed."

"What are you going to do?" Haakon asked. "Things were going to be hard enough with you bringing a woman home, but a man? Do you think the clan will even accept him?"

"Do they have a choice?" Radulfr replied. "I don't remember having to get their permission to wed or their approval of who I wed."

"No, but…" Haakon reached up and rubbed the back of his neck as he gazed at Ein. "I just don't know how they are going to take this, him."

"You know as well as I do what will happen if I break the *handsal*. Our clan and all of its members will be outcasts, just as if a *geas* had been placed upon us."

"And you don't think bringing a man home as your bride will not bring a curse down upon us anyway?" Haakon waved his hand at Ein. "He's a man, Radulfr. Your bride is a man."

"You keep saying that like you expect it to suddenly change," Radulfr said.

"Radulfr!"

"Why do you hate me so much?" Ein whispered from beside Radulfr. "I've wronged you in no way. I've never even met you."

"Look, I don't hate you, Ein" Haakon said. He dropped his hands to his waist and blew out a deep breath. "I'm just worried about what bringing you home will do to our clan. There's enough pain and grief there now because of your brother."

"Half brother, and I've never even met Fafnir."

"Fine, your half brother, but that still doesn't change the fact that there is going to be an upheaval if Radulfr brings you home."

"I do not know how to alleviate your worry. I do not plan to cause trouble nor do I have animosity toward you or your clan. I can only promise to follow the dictates of the *handsal* and hope that I will be accepted."

"And you think that's going to fix things?" Haakon snapped. "People aren't going to want to have anything to do with you. Hell, I doubt they will even want to speak to you."

"Would you prefer that I didn't speak with you?" Ein asked. Radulfr could feel trembling beneath the hand he had on Ein's arm, but the man hid it well. "I am sure whatever curse my being a man brings down from the gods will not affect you if we have no close association."

Haakon looked as if his head might explode. His face was turning a motley red, his lips pressed firmly together. Radulfr would have interfered and defended Ein except he seemed to be doing a pretty damn good job of doing it himself.

Besides, he knew Haakon didn't really have an issue with the fact that Ein was a man. Haakon had been with a few in his time as well. He was just worried about their clan and what their reaction would be to Ein's arrival.

"Ein, I didn't mean to say that you yourself are a curse. I just… I'm worried, and if you knew anything about what is going on, you would understand why I'm worried."

"It was explained to me what Fafnir did. I do understand your concern. I have much the same concerns myself, but I cannot change who I am or how this *hansal* came about. I can only accept it and hope to honor the agreement as it was stated."

Haakon threw his hands up in the air. "Fine, go, be merry. There is apparently nothing I can do to make you see reason."

"Do you still wish for me not to talk to you?"

"No, talking to me is fine. I imagine we will be spending a lot of time talking together in the future." Haakon chuckled and gestured to Radulfr. "He's not an easy man to get to know. I'm sure you're going to need my help keeping him under control."

"I'd appreciate the help."

Radulfr didn't know what to make of Ein's mischievous little smile or the somewhat odd pact that seemed to have just formed between Haakon and Ein before his very eyes. He couldn't think of two men that were further apart on the spectrum than Haakon and Ein, unless he threw Vadirr into the mix.

Vadirr didn't have a delicate bone in his body. Radulfr was strong. Vadirr was stronger. The only reason he hadn't been made jarl was simply because he didn't want the position. If he did, and ever challenged for leadership, Radulfr didn't know which one of them would win. He didn't want to find out either.

"All right, introductions have been made," Radulfr said, pulling Ein to his side. "We still need to complete the required rituals of the *handsal* before we can head for home."

Vadirr chuckled. "You mean you still need to claim your betrothed."

Radulfr grinned. "There is that."

Chapter 4

Ein felt so anxious his stomach twisted together in knots. He sat curled under a pile of furs on his platform in the *byre* waiting for Radulfr to join him. And he was butt-ass naked. It didn't get anymore nerve-racking than that.

He could hear people talking and laughing outside his door and knew that they would be coming in at any moment. He just wished that he had a little more time getting to know Radulfr or at least talking with him before the big show.

The very thought that not only would Radulfr be coming into the room in a moment, but six other men who would watch them have sex, made Ein grip the furs in his hands so tight that his knuckles turned white.

He was scared enough about his performance during sex with Radulfr considering that he'd never had sex before. Add in the witnesses and Ein wasn't sure he was going to be able to do anything but lie there. He was terrified.

When the door opened and Radulfr stepped inside, Ein scooted up closer to the head of his bed and swallowed hard. It suddenly felt hard to breathe, like there wasn't enough air in the room to take in.

"How are you doing, Ein?" Radulfr asked softly as if his words were just for Ein and not the men still standing outside. "Are you ready for this?"

Ein started shaking his head no until he realized what he was doing. He swallowed again. "I think so."

Radulfr smiled as he walked across the room to sit on the side of the bed next to Ein. He reached down and gently patted Ein's leg. Ein saw it coming, but the touch of Radulfr's hand on his body, even through the furs, was still enough to make him jump. "It'll be okay, Ein, I promise. There's not much to this."

"I'm not sure if that's a good thing or not." Ein laughed nervously.

"I wanted a few minutes with you before the others came in to make sure you were ready for what is about to happen." Ein didn't jump this time when Radulfr patted his leg again and thought maybe he wasn't quite so nervous now that Radulfr was here. "Do you have any questions about what is going to happen?"

"Do they really have to watch us?" That's the part Ein was most nervous about. "I'm not sure I can pretend they're not in the room."

"You let me worry about that. I have no doubt I'll be able to keep you plenty distracted."

Ein was dying of curiosity to know what Radulfr meant. He knew the basics of sex. He'd seen enough farm animals copulate to know what was done. He just didn't know how things were done between two people exactly.

"Will it hurt?"

"It might, but I'll try to make sure there isn't too much pain. The more we come together, the less it will hurt."

"This witnessing thing, do they have to actually watch us or do they just have to be in the room? I mean, can we cover up with a fur or something?"

"Unfortunately, no. The witnesses must see me claim you in order for the requirements of the *handsal* to be completed. If we were hiding under the furs, we could later say that we faked it and nothing really happened, thus nullifying the *handsal*. The witnesses wouldn't be able to say otherwise."

"So…" Ein felt his face start to pale, "they actually have to see it?"

"It?" Radulfr chuckled. "Yes, Ein, they have to actually see me fuck you in the ass."

Ein felt his face go from cold and clammy to burning hot in a split second. He gripped the fur in his hands tighter and pulled it up to his neck. He absently noticed that his hands were trembling and tried to hide them under the covers.

"Ein." Radulfr's voice was whisper-soft as he reached for Ein's hands. "I promise it won't be as bad as you think. You'll hardly even notice that they are in the room." Radulfr chuckled suddenly. "Well, at least I hope you will be too distracted to notice."

"Ho–how do we do this?"

"You mean how do two men have sex together?"

Ein shrugged, too embarrassed to put voice to what he was asking.

"You don't know?"

"Not exactly."

Ein's panic started to set in when Radulfr grabbed the furs covering his naked body and started slowly pulling on them. "What are you doing?"

Radulfr's amused smirk made Ein nervous. "I think it would be better if I showed you rather than told you."

"Sh–show me?" Ein slapped his hand over his mouth when his voice started to squeak. He felt like an idiot, especially when Radulfr pulled the fur farther down and exposed him, a low growl coming from the man.

The fur down around his feet, Ein watched in rapt anticipation as Radulfr moved to kneel on the platform bed, slowly crawling up to cover him with his larger body. Ein felt the air leave his lungs when Radulfr settled over him, but he couldn't seem to draw anymore back in.

"Radulfr," he panted when the man seemed to just be watching him. Radulfr didn't make any move toward him other than pressing their bodies together. He didn't touch or caress or kiss. He just stared until Ein began to grow anxious. "What's wrong?"

"Do you have any idea how truly beautiful you are?"

"Me?" He was squeaking again.

"Yes, you." Radulfr chuckled. "I know men are supposed to be manly and handsome, but you are more beautiful than most women I know."

Ein frowned, not sure how he was supposed to answer that. "I'm sorry?"

"I'm not. I think I will enjoy looking at you for the next sixty years."

"Just sixty?"

"Well…" Radulfr finally moved, his hand cupping around the side of Ein's face. "I hope for more, but we live in dangerous times. There's no telling what might happen to either of us. If we're lucky, we'll have many years together."

"I'd prefer it."

Radulfr grinned. "Me, too."

Ein's breath caught in his throat when Radulfr leaned down and kissed him. This was only the second kiss he'd ever received in his life, and it was just as earth-shattering as the first one. Ein found it particularly interesting that they had both happened on the same day and came from the same man. That had to mean something.

Right?

Radulfr's lips pressed against his felt wonderful. If the tingling Ein felt in the pit of his stomach was any indication of what sex with Radulfr was like, Ein could only hope they did it often.

Radulfr kept one hand curved around Ein's face, but before he knew it, the other one was moving down his body. Ein didn't know whether to be disturbed by the sensations racking his body or embrace them. He did know that Radulfr's touch left a path of aching skin in his wake.

When Radulfr's lips began to move away from his mouth and along the edge of his jawline, Ein arched his head back to give the man better access. He tried to swallow, but Radulfr's teeth gently latched on to the soft swell of Ein's Adam's apple, leaving a small ache in its place as he moved on.

Ein's entire body shuddered when Radulfr's tongue traced the soft shell of his ear, moving up to the pointed tip then back down to the small lobe. Ein groaned, the sensation of Radulfr's hot breath blowing across his ear almost more than he could stand.

"Do you know you're ears are pointed, Ein?" Radulfr whispered.

Ein nodded. "Al–always been that way."

"It's very cute."

Cute?

Ein blinked, frowning at Radulfr's words. He didn't mind being called beautiful so much, but cute? He started to open his mouth to protest, only to have it filled with Radulfr's tongue as the man kissed him again. He forgot his objection almost immediately, kissing Radulfr back.

Radulfr pulled away from the kiss suddenly and moved down to wrap his lips around Ein's nipple. Ein cried out and arched up into the air, never having felt a sensation so intense before in his life. Even Radulfr's kiss didn't compare to the ecstasy Ein felt at the touch of the man's mouth on his body.

Ein reached up to grab a handful of Radulfr's hair, wanting to hold him closer. He never wanted the pleasure shooting through his body to end. And he didn't think it could get any better until he felt Radulfr's fingers slip between his butt cheeks.

Ein froze, holding his breath as an oil-slicked finger slowly pushed into him, breaching him for the very first time. The sensation wasn't unpleasant, but it wasn't the mind-boggling one he felt when Radulfr kissed him.

He glanced down to find Radulfr watching him intently even though his lips continued to explore his naked flesh. When a second finger breached him, Ein inhaled sharply at the burn of pain he felt at the intrusion. It still wasn't earth-shattering. Ein would rather be kissing Radulfr.

"Breathe, *kisa*."

Breathe. Yeah, right.

Ein nodded rapidly. He tried to draw in a deep breath, but just as he did, Radulfr pushed a third finger into him. Ein cried out. His legs dropped open even farther as he tried to get more of Radulfr's fingers into his tight entrance. He had felt something, a spark of pleasure that blew away every other sensation he'd ever felt, and he wanted to feel it again.

"Wha–what was that?"

"That's what makes this so wonderful, *kisa*."

Ein had no idea what Radulfr was talking about, but he knew he liked it when the man started moving his fingers around, pushing them in and out of his ass. Ein started moving with Radlufr, pushing back.

"Radulfr," he moaned.

"Soon, *kisa*."

Ein nodded, although he wasn't sure what he was agreeing to. He just knew he never wanted to stop. When Radulfr moved to kneel between his legs and flipped him over onto his stomach, Ein wanted to protest. He liked what Radulfr had been doing.

Then he felt something press against his ass again, something warm and hard but silky soft at the same time. Radulfr's hands gripped his hips as Ein was slowly filled. His breath came and went in quick little pants.

"Ah, sweet hell, Ein, you feel so good," Radulfr groaned into Ein's ear as he leaned over him.

Ein arched his back, pressing up into the large body covering him. Radulfr felt just as good, if not better. He had never felt anything like it in his life. The feeling of Radulfr's cock filling his ass was far better than kissing, although that was good, too.

And then Radulfr started to move, and every intelligent thought Ein had in his mind melted away. Ein planted his hands and knees in the mattress and pushed back as Radulfr thrust forward. He couldn't seem to get enough of Radulfr.

The sensations riding over him made his skin prickle. Ein could even feel the hairs on the nape of his neck standing on end. There seemed to be a spot inside of him that Radulfr's cock rubbed against every time the man thrust forward. It made Ein cry out.

He almost opened his mouth to beg for more. And he would have until he felt a hand wrap around his cock, and then nothing came out of his mouth except the air left in his lungs. He could barely breathe after that, just feel.

Radulfr became more fierce, pounding into Ein so much so that the platform creaked. Ein didn't care. Each movement, each thrust of Radulfr's body against his, in his, felt wonderful to Ein. He never wanted it to end.

But then the sensations building in his body seemed to suddenly pool in his groin, in the hand wrapped around his cock stroking him and the cock pounding into his ass. Ein cried out as his world exploded into a million glowing stars. His vision seemed to blur from the brightness as he came.

A muted roar came from behind Ein, warning him a split second before Radulfr's hot release filled his ass. Ein dropped his head down onto the furs beneath him and closed his eyes, breathing heavily as he rode out his orgasm.

He barely registered Radulfr pulling away and covering them both with the furs on the bed. Strong arms wrapped around him and pulled him over onto his side. He just felt too melted to acknowledge anything.

"Will that suffice?"

Except that.

Ein frowned, Radulfr's words breaking into the euphoric bubble he floated in. He opened his eyes, inhaling swiftly when he saw several men standing around the room watching them. Ein groaned, quickly closing his eyes again before burying his face in the furs.

He had been so wrapped up in the sensations raging through his body that he hadn't even realized the witnesses had come into the room. He was so embarrassed. He doubted he would be able to look any of these men in the face ever again.

"If you're satisfied that the requirements of the *handsal* have been met, I'd like some time alone with my mate."

Ein would be forever grateful for Radulfr's words as he heard the men leave the room, the door shutting quietly behind them. Once the door was closed, Ein felt Radulfr cuddle up behind him, an arm dropping over his waist.

"Are you okay, Ein?"

Ein opened his eyes and turned his head to look back at Radulfr, nodding even though he could feel his face flush. "I'm fine."

"Did I hurt you?"

"No." Ein could feel his face heat up even more as he turned away, facing forward. Ein couldn't say that the sensations he had felt were painful exactly, mind-blowing and exhilarating, maybe, but not painful. "I'm good, I promise."

"You'll tell me if you're not?"

"Yes."

"Did I distract you enough?"

Ein rolled his eyes when he heard the amusement in Radulfr's voice. "Looking for a compliment?"

"No, not really." Radulfr chuckled. "I really just wanted to make sure you enjoyed yourself."

"You know I did."

"Want to see if you enjoy it a second time?"

"Can we?" Ein turned to look back over his shoulder at Radulfr.

"We've completed the requirements of the *handsal*, Ein. We can do anything we want."

"But we haven't," Ein protested. "We didn't exchange rings."

"Easily fixed, *kisa*."

Ein frowned when Radulfr rolled over and reached for something on the floor. He was even more confused when Radulfr pulled his pants up to the bed. "I wondered where those went. I never even felt you pull them off."

Radulfr chuckled. "That's a good thing. It means you were enjoying yourself."

"Apparently enough not to notice six other men in the room," Ein said as he flopped back on the pillows. He chuckled when a stray duck feather puffed up into the air from the pillow then slowly floated down.

"That's what I wanted. While having the witnesses there was a must, I wanted you to have good memories of our first time together. I could see how nervous you were."

Ein nodded. He had been nervous.

"Here."

Ein glanced down to see Radulfr holding something. He held out his hand, pushing himself up onto his elbows when Radulfr dropped a silver ring into the palm of his hand. "Where did you get this?"

"I brought them with me."

"Them?" Ein glanced away from the ring in his hand to see Radulfr holding one exactly like it between two fingers.

"My *faðir* told me to have these made the day I came of age. He said one day I would find my betrothed and I would need a symbol of my commitment." Radulfr shrugged. "I'm pretty sure he was talking about a woman, but I think maybe I was envisioning something else."

"What makes you say that?"

"Well, the ring you hold fits my finger perfectly. I know this because I've tried it on a few times." Radulfr nodded toward the ring in his hand. "This ring is its twin, made at the very same time. When I got it back from the jeweler, I was upset because it wasn't the delicate ring I had envisioned would grace the finger of my bride. It was bigger."

Ein looked closer at the ring, narrowing his eyes. "It's bigger?"

"I wanted to beat the jeweler into the ground for messing up the ring I would give my betrothed, but my *faðir* said I couldn't. He said it was made the size it was for a reason, that the gods knew what they were doing and I needed to just accept it, that it would fit the finger of the betrothed that the gods chose for me." Radulfr reached over and grabbed Ein's free hand, sliding the ring onto his finger. "See, a perfect fit."

* * * *

Ein covered his mouth as he tried to stifle yet another yawn. Radulfr said they needed to get up early to get started back to his homestead, but Ein had no idea early meant before the sun came up. Hell, the sun wasn't even thinking about coming up yet. That wouldn't happen for another few hours.

He doubted he had gotten more than a couple of hours of sleep after he and Radulfr made love one more time before closing their eyes. Seeing his ring gracing Ein's finger seemed to give Radulfr added enthusiasm. Ein still felt a little sore from the pounding he'd received, but he wouldn't have traded it for anything in the world.

Radulfr seemed to know just what to do, just where to touch Ein to make him lose his mind. The second time they came together, Ein had come twice. He was interested to see what would happen the third time. He just might pass out.

"How are you doing, Ein?"

Ein glanced over at Radulfr and smiled. They had been riding for a while now. As tired as he was, Ein also felt excited. He was seeing land that he had never seen before. "I'm okay."

"We'll travel for a few more hours then camp by the river just at the base of that mountain range before the sun sets."

Ein followed the direction Radulfr pointed and suddenly felt more excited about their trip. "Is that snow?"

"Yes."

"Where is your home from here?"

"Our home, Ein."

Ein chuckled. "Okay, where is *our* home from here?"

"Believe it or not, on the other side of those mountains."

"We get to go through the snow?"

"We'll see some of it, yes, but we won't be going up over the mountain range. There's a small valley pass on the other side of the river. We'll go through that until we reach the other side of the mountains, and then it's just another few days before we reach our home."

Ein could barely make out the green trees on the side of the mountain. They had to be miles away. He couldn't even begin to imagine how far Radulfr's home was from where they were now.

"How soon until it snows at home?"

"We should have another month at least before the snow begins to fall. After that, it depends on the gods."

Ein couldn't wait. He had heard about snow. He'd even seen it off in the distance. He'd just never actually touched it. Having lived all of his life at the *hov*, Ein experienced a wide range of weather, everything from freezing rain to blistering hot summers. Snow would be a new experience.

"We should be home in about a week, depending on weather and barring any problems."

"A week?"

He knew once they arrived at their destination, Radulfr's time would be taken up with the clan and they wouldn't have much time together. Ein was excited about seeing his new home, but he also wanted some time to spend alone with Radulfr before they reached it. A week would do just fine.

Chapter 5

Radulfr couldn't believe how anxious he felt as they set up camp for the night. He was unloading the horses while others set up camp. Haakon had gotten Ein's help to start a fire while Vadirr and a couple of the others hunted for their nightly meal.

Even though Ein was just feet from him, Radulfr couldn't help but search him out every few minutes. He hadn't been able to stop looking at Ein since the first moment he met him. The man truly was stunning. Radulfr couldn't figure out how no one else had seen it before now and snapped him up. The men at the *hov* must have been blind.

Knowing that Ein now belonged to him made Radulfr feel very satisfied with how things turned out. He would have accepted a woman as his betrothed, but he was actually pretty damn happy Ein was a man.

It also made him want to growl every time Haakon moved too close to Ein. There was a possessiveness growing in Radulfr that he wasn't sure he was prepared to deal with. He'd never felt possessive over someone before. Trysts were forgotten almost as soon as they were over.

Radulfr hadn't been able to stop thinking about the previous night since he woke up. He'd spent the better part of the day with a hard-on. Even now, just watching Ein laugh and move around the fire made Radulfr ache.

He was glad they were finally making camp for the night because he didn't know how much longer he could keep his hands off of Ein. He just hoped the night went quickly. There wouldn't be much that they could do considering that everyone would be sleeping around the fire, but that didn't mean they couldn't have a quick rub off together.

"He really is a looker, isn't he?"

Radulfr growled and turned to glare at Vidarr. He knew Ein was as sexy as any man he had ever seen. He just didn't want others talking about Ein, especially not in a sexual manner. No one should even be thinking of Ein in a sexual manner.

"And what if he is?" Radulfr asked.

"I'm just saying…"

"Well, don't."

Vidarr held his hands up in front of him. "I wouldn't dream of it."

Radulfr sighed. He knew he was being totally unreasonable. Vidarr hadn't said anything wrong. He hadn't even done anything wrong. Radulfr just didn't like anyone looking at Ein. Anyone looking at the man could instantly tell how beautiful he was.

"We caught a couple of rabbits," Vidarr said. "Haakon is getting them ready right now. They shouldn't take too long to cook. I thought maybe you'd like to take Ein down to the creek to wash up while the meat is cooking."

Radulfr glanced up in surprise. He hadn't expected that. "Yes, I would. Thank you, my friend."

Vidarr shrugged as if his gesture meant nothing, but Radulfr knew that it did. They were warriors, *vikingr*. They fought hard, and they lived even harder. It wasn't in them to be gentle. The show of compassion for one weaker than them wasn't often seen.

Their honor may have demanded that they protect those weaker than them, but they lived in a world filled with danger. Being weak wasn't allowed. As such, most of them had learned to never show emotion or compassion. They needed to be battle-ready at all times.

For Vidarr to recognize Ein's need for a gentle hand was so unusual that Radulfr was a little shocked. But he couldn't say he wasn't pleased. Ein did need a gentle hand. He wasn't a battle-ridden warrior.

"I'll escort Ein to the creek. We shouldn't be long."

Vidarr placed his hand on the hilt of his sword. "I'll keep watch."

Radulfr nodded then glanced across to campsite to the two warriors who had accompanied them from Jarl Dagr's clan. They were taking their gear off their horses and setting it by the fire. Radulfr gestured toward them with his head, trying to look casual.

"Keep an eye on those two," he said. "I don't trust them."

"I don't either." Vidarr's hand tightened on his sword handle as he glowered in the two men's direction. "Anyone in the service of Jarl Dagr isn't worth the dirt to bury them."

"Well, don't start anything if you can help it. I don't need the aggravation. The lawspeaker would be pretty upset if we had to kill two of Jarl Dagr's men." Radulfr chuckled lightly. "He'd understand it, but he'd still be upset."

"Understood."

Radulfr knew his orders would be followed. Vidarr and Haakon were his right and left hands. They were his counsel, his advice-givers. The guarded his back, his sides, and his front. They gave Radulfr their complete loyalty. Radulfr trusted them more than he trusted anyone.

"*Kisa*, come." Radulfr gestured with his hand as he walked toward his mate. "We're going down to the creek to wash before the rabbit is done. Grab whatever you need out of your bag."

Ein's face lit up as he turned to look at Radulfr. "Really?"

Radulfr cocked an eyebrow.

Ein's face flushed, and he hurried to grab his bag. Radulfr followed Ein with his eyes until heard a muffled snicker. He instantly swung back to glare at the two soldiers sent by Jarl Dagr.

"You have something to say?"

Both men glared for a moment then dropped their eyes under Radulfr's intense stare. Radulfr expected as much. He wasn't a jarl in his own right for nothing. He'd learned before he was ten winters old how to stare warriors down, a trait taught to him by his *faðir*.

"I'm ready."

Radulfr turned away from the two men to see Ein standing beside him, a bundle of cloth held in his arms. The corner of Radulfr's mouth lifted up in amusement. Ein was practically bouncing in place. Radulfr grabbed Ein's arm and guided him away from the camp toward the woods.

The creek they were headed to was quite a ways from the camp, and the forest was pretty thick. They would only travel toward home during the daylight hours from here on out. The woods were safer during the day—less chance of an ambush.

"I want you to stay away from those two warriors, Ein."

"Why?"

"Because I said so," Radulfr growled. He wasn't used to having his orders questioned. His warriors and those in his clan never questioned him or disobeyed an order. It was part of the whole jarl thing.

"Okay," Ein whispered.

Radulfr rolled his eyes. "They are in the service of Jarl Dagr. I don't trust them."

"Why didn't you just say that then?"

Radulfr jerked on Ein's arm, pulling him to a stop. "Ein, I am jarl. I do not need to explain myself to you. If I give you an order, I expect you to follow it. No questions asked."

"Ohhhkay."

To Radulfr's annoyance, he found the corner's of his lips threatening to curl up in a smile. "You're going to lead me on a merry chase, aren't you?" he asked with a heavy irony. He knew he was doomed when Ein grinned.

Radulfr sighed and started leading Ein toward the creek again. It took longer to reach their destination than he liked. Ein, having lived in the *hov* all of his life, definitely was not used to walking through the woods.

"Be quick, Ein," he said once they reached the water's edge. Radulfr stepped over to the base of a large tree trunk and squatted down. He pulled out a small dagger and began whittling a piece of wood.

Radulfr kept one eye on the surrounding area and one on Ein. He barely glanced down at the wood he was carving. He had spent years honing his skills as a warrior. One of them was looking casual while being on guard. He was an expert at it.

He was impressed with the quickness in which Ein washed up. None of the man's movements were wasted. He unfolded his little bundle, took off his shirt, and washed up. Once he was done, he put on a clean shirt and bundled his dirty items back up. He took maybe ten minutes from start to finish.

"Okay, I'm done," Ein said as he turned back around to face Radulfr.

His eyes suddenly widened, showing the tortured dullness of disbelief and growing fear. Radulfr was puzzled by Ein's abrupt change of mood. He had seemed so happy just seconds before.

A cold knot formed in his stomach when Ein started to shake. He dropped the dagger and reached for the handle of his sword. He tried not to swallow when he felt the cold hard press of a sharp blade against his throat.

"Pull it out slowly, jarl. No sudden movements."

Radulfr kept his eyes on Ein as he slowly pulled his sword out of its leather scabbard. Ein breathed in shallow quick gasps, but he hadn't moved from his spot. He hadn't even dropped his bundle of clothing.

The sword was jerked out of Radulfr's hand. He heard it crash into the brush a moment later. The sword tip in his neck moved, pushing against his skin.

"Now, slowly get to your feet, jarl."

Radulfr did as the man asked. Fury almost choked him when he saw the abject fear in Ein's eyes. It slowly turned to a scalding fury as

Ein continued to shake. He wasn't quite sure who held him at sword point, but he planned to find out—after he killed him.

"The three of us are going to take a little walk," the man said. He moved the sword away from Radulfr's neck and pressed the tip into the middle of his back. "Move real slowly and don't try anything stupid. My friends are waiting for us and will come at the first sound of trouble."

"Why are you doing this?" Radulfr asked as he started walking forward. He really had no idea where they were headed, but he knew he couldn't allow either himself or Ein to be taken farther into the woods. He didn't know who might be waiting for them.

"Because the money is so damn good." The man laughed. "I'll live like a king."

Radulfr tilted his head just enough to catch a shock of brown hair out of the corner of his eye. If this man got away for any reason, Radulfr wanted to be able to track him down.

He didn't like the direction they were taking, which was right toward his mate. He didn't want this man anywhere close to Ein. As he walked, he started turning his steps heading off to the side of Ein. He just hoped Ein stayed put.

"You're a mercenary?"

Radulfr grunted and stumbled forward when the blade in his back jabbed him. He could feel blood start to trickle down his back and knew the man had pierced his skin. Apparently he didn't like what Radulfr said.

"I am a warrior," the man snapped.

"Warriors live by a code of honor. They do not assassinate people for silver coins."

"What do you know about it? You're a jarl. You've never had to wonder where your next meal is coming from."

Radulfr clenched his teeth. "I am a jarl because I hold my honor close to me."

Radulfr was suddenly pushed forward. He staggered several steps then caught himself on a large boulder. His breathe seemed to solidify in his throat when he heard Ein cry out. He choked back a cry when he turned and saw Ein being held against a larger man, a sword across his throat.

"Do you hold this close as well?" the mercenary asked.

Radulfr tried to keep his heart cold and still as he looked into the eyes of the man that held Ein. He hoped the man saw his death when he looked back at him because it was coming. The muscles of Radulfr's forearm hardened as he tensed.

He cast a quick look at Ein then clenched his jaw when he saw a tear rolled down Ein's cheek. His smoky gray eyes clawed at Radulfr like talons, tearing the last shred of his control away and burning them to cinders.

"You will die slowly." Radulfr threw the words at the mercenary like stones. There was no wiggle room. He would grant no mercy. "No one holds a weapon against Ein's throat and lives."

Radulfr's heart hammered in his chest. His breathing was ragged. He hands clenched with the need to kill the man holding Ein. The fury he felt at the sight of the blade across Ein's throat grew until he felt his skin crawl.

His head roared with the need for the mercenary's death until all he could see was red. His teeth started chattering. He shivered and clenched his hands, wincing when they cut into the palms of his hands.

He could see the fear growing in the mercenary's eyes. The man could see his own death coming. He started backing away, taking Ein with him. Radulfr felt a burning itch in his skin the farther away they moved. He felt his muscles spasm.

Radulfr growled and lunged. Ein dropped to the ground. Radulfr went right over the top of him and took the mercenary down. His hands clawed at the man, ripping away at his clothes until he felt flesh beneath his fingers.

He distantly heard a horrific screaming, but it gave him satisfaction more than anything. Blinding fury ripped through Radulfr as he tore and shredded the flesh beneath his fingers. He destroyed until the bloodlust swarming through his body had been appeased.

Radulfr suddenly stopped, panting heavily. He shook his head to rid himself of a persistent buzzing sound that seemed to drown everything else out. When his mind cleared, Radulfr heard muffled whimpering.

He turned toward the frightened sound. His eyes narrowed when he spotted Ein crouched against a tree. The man's eyes were rounded, slightly dazed. His body trembled. Radulfr pushed himself away from the mercenary. He needed to get to his mate.

He had started to crawl toward Ein when his strength gave way and he fell to hard ground. He tried to push himself up. Radulfr groaned when his arms gave out and he hit the ground again. He lay there for a minute, his body aching, and tried to catch his breath.

When Radulfr tried to get up again, he could barely lift his head. He was so exhausted he dropped back down to the ground. He shivered against the coldness that suddenly seemed to fill the air, his body chilled nearly to the bone.

"Radulfr?"

Radulfr turned his head when he felt something brush his cheek. Ein was kneeling beside him. He reached out with his hand and laid it on Ein's thigh.

"Ein," he whispered with the last of his strength. His eyes started to close as exhaustion claimed his body. "I–I'm sorry."

* * * *

Ein knew the moment Radulfr passed out. The man's huge body slumped to the ground. Ein bit his bottom lip and looked around anxiously as he tried to figure out what to do. He wasn't a warrior. He didn't fight. He wouldn't even know how to.

A shudder racked Ein's body when his eyes fell on the bloody mess of the man that attacked them. Ein recognized him as one of Jarl Dagr's soldiers, but that was only because he had seen the man before Radulfr attacked him. Now, he was just a bloody mass of flesh and bones.

Ein didn't understand what had happened to Radulfr. He didn't even want to think about it. He just couldn't seem to stop. Radulfr seemed fine now except for being unconscious. He didn't have long sharp teeth or dark black fur. Even the claws had receded.

Ein couldn't remember being so scared in his life. Radulfr had transformed into something not human. Even his body had changed, growing larger, more muscular. Hell, his eyes had glowed.

Ein twisted his hands together. Every fiber of his body told him to run and run fast. He just couldn't leave Radulfr unprotected. He'd never forgive himself if something happened to the man while he couldn't take care of himself.

Ein realized what he was thinking at the same time he realized he had already made his decision to stay. He had to protect Radulfr until he could protect himself. Ein pushed himself to his feet and went in search of weapons.

He found Radulfr's sword in the bushes. He found the dagger Radulfr had been carving with at the base of a tree. The mercenary's sword, luckily, was a few feet away from his gnarled body. Ein gathered all of the weapons together in a pile next to Radulfr's body.

Radulfr's clothes seemed to be shredded rags, just hanging on his body now that he had returned to his previous size. Ein used his dirty clothes to cover Radulfr's nearly naked body then huddled closer to share his body warmth. He just hoped Radulfr woke soon. He was scared, cold, and hungry. He wanted to go home.

The lack of noise freaked Ein out. He could hear the creek trickling and the occasional blow of wind through the trees, but other than that, there was nothing. There wasn't even any wildlife. It was eerie.

Ein slowly grew used to the silence, though, so when he heard another noise, he was suddenly alert. He sat up and looked around, his heart pounding frantically in his chest. Nothing moved in the trees or underlying brush.

Ein knew he had heard something. He continued to search the forest for danger as he reached over and grabbed Radulfr's sword and pulled it up close to his chest, gripping it tightly with both hands.

Glowing eyes appeared in the bushes. Ein gulped and scooted closer to Radulfr. A shiver of fear swept through him as the eyes began to move closer. Ein jumped and turned when he heard a noise behind him only to find more glowing eyes staring out through the woods.

"Radulfr," Ein whispered as he nudged the man. "Radulfr, wake up."

The clouds overhead suddenly parted and bathed the small area with moonlight. When Ein looked around, he realized that he and Radulfr were surrounded by a pack of wolves—wolves with glowing eyes.

"Radulfr." Ein reached over and shook Radulfr's shoulder. "Please, you have to wake up."

Radulfr didn't move.

Ein's breath caught in his throat as the wolves started walking out of the trees and bushes. He couldn't move any closer to Radulfr unless he climbed on top of the man.

"Please, stay back," Ein cried out as he swung the sword around. He was a little surprised at how light the sword was. He had seen Radulfr handle it and thought it was much bigger. It looked much bigger. But he seemed to be able to swing it with ease.

The wolf right in front of Ein, the largest of them, suddenly dropped down to his stomach then started crawling forward. Ein frowned, confused. The sword in his hand started to waver. The wolf whimpered and crawled forward a bit more.

Ein froze, not moving a single finger as he watched the wolf crawl up to Radulfr and start sniffing his long black hair. Ein slowly lowered the sword and glanced around. His eyebrows shot up when he saw that all of the wolves were on the ground, surrounding them.

Not a single one of them made a threatening gesture. They just lay there, watching Radulfr. Eerie didn't even begin to describe the scene. Ein tensed when the large wolf in front of him whimpered and nudged Radulfr. He seemed almost concerned.

"He's going to be okay," Ein whispered.

He blinked in surprise when he realized that he was trying to comfort a wolf. Strangely enough, the wolf lifted his head and stared up at Ein then leaned forward and gently licked the top of his hand where it rested around the hilt of Radulfr's sword.

Ein nearly jumped out of his skin when the wolves suddenly stood up and moved closer. He just knew they were going to be eaten alive. His hands tightened on the sword handle. When the wolves just stepped closer and lay back down, Ein breathed a sigh of relief.

He and Radulfr were totally surrounded, the warm fur of the wolves pressing up against him and Radulfr, keeping them warm. All of the wolves except the largest one tucked their heads into their bodies and closed their eyes. They looked like they were going to sleep.

The largest one drew Ein's attention when he suddenly sat up, but he just sat there, not making a move. Ein wasn't even sure he blinked. Then the wolf started turning his head, slowly looking one way then the other. Every few minutes he lifted his nose into the air, his nostrils flaring as he sniffed the air, and then he would go back to looking around.

"You're on guard duty, aren't you?"

Ein had no idea how he knew what the wolf was doing or even why he had said it out loud, but when the wolf turned to look at him, Ein could swear that he saw a spark of intelligence in his glowing eyes.

For some reason Ein didn't want to pursue too strongly the knowledge that he and Radulfr were being guarded made him feel better. He knew that Radulfr's warriors would come for them when they didn't return, but he felt safer knowing he wasn't trying to guard Radulfr all by himself.

Ein placed the sword on the ground next to him and curled his body closer to Radulfr. He heard a little yip come from the largest wolf then warm fur pressed against him from the back and side as two of the other wolves pressed closer to him.

The situation was absurd, but Ein was too relieved to laugh. He was lost in the woods, his mate unconscious, and he was being warmed and guarded by a pack of intelligent wolves with glowing eyes. Maybe his Uncle Loki was playing games with him?

Chapter 6

Radulfr's head felt like it was going to explode. He groaned and reached up to cradle his head in his hands. He couldn't remember having a headache like this before, not even when he fell off his horse and got trampled during a battle.

He started to push himself up when he suddenly came face to face with a large dark-gray wolf. Radulfr swallowed hard and tried not to move. He even tried not to breathe. The wolf seemed huge, much bigger than any other wolf Radulfr had ever seen.

"Good doggie."

Radulfr eyes widened when the wolf literally rolled his eyes. So, that wasn't supposed to happen. First off, wolves shouldn't be able to roll their eyes. Second, how in the hell did the wolf even know what he was saying?

"Uh, I'm just going to sit up now," Radulfr said as he slowly pushed back from the wolf. He made sure all of his movements were gradual and deliberate. He didn't want to spook the wolf and suddenly find himself with a throat full of sharp teeth.

As soon as he stood up, the wolf stepped back and sat on his haunches. He just seemed to be watching Radulfr, almost as if he were curious. Radulfr stared back at the wolf, wondering why he didn't feel any danger. He could always feel danger before it happened. It was like a sixth sense that he had, that he depended on. It never steered him wrong before.

Radulfr decided to respect his sixth sense and not reach for a weapon. He would trust that the wolf was merely curious and not a danger. That didn't mean he wouldn't keep a close eye on the wolf, because he would. Another thing he relied on was never letting his guard down.

"Radulfr?"

Radulfr turned. He was never so grateful to see someone in his life. He grabbed Ein and crushed the little man to his chest. He bent down and buried his face in Ein's neck, drawing in the man's strong scent. He didn't remember Ein smelling so sweet before. He inhaled deeper, nuzzling his face deeper into the curve of Ein's neck until the man giggled.

"What are you doing?"

"You smell really good, Ein."

Radulfr couldn't seem to get enough. He wanted to inhale Ein, roll in his scent. It was the most divine scent he had ever smelled. The harder he inhaled, the harder his cock became, like there was a direct connection between the way Ein smelled and how aroused Radulfr was. It was agonizing, exquisite.

"Radulfr, you can't," Ein whispered even as the man tilted his head away to bare his throat. "They're watching."

Radulfr reluctantly pulled away from Ein when he heard a sharp yip. He kept his arms wrapped around Ein as he turned to look at the large gray wolf. The wolf sat there watching intently, his tongue hanging out of his mouth.

Radulfr didn't know how, but he knew the wolf could smell his arousal. He felt his face flush a little. The feeling of embarrassment was not something he was used to. He wagged his finger at the wolf.

"Don't even think about it," he said. "You don't get to watch."

Radulfr could swear the wolf looked disappointed as he sank back down to the ground and rested his head on his paws. Radulfr shook his head as he glanced around and realized that he and Ein were surrounded by wolves. He also realized it was light out. The last thing he remembered was the darkness and...

Radulfr's heart suddenly hammered in his chest. He noticed the wolf jump up and start looking around as well as if on guard. It was unnerving but not as much as the mass of skin and bones in a pile several feet away.

"By Thor's hammer!"

"What?" Ein glanced around wildly.

"That!" Radulfr pointed to the dead body. "What is that?"

Ein slumped against his chest. "You scared me there for a minute."

"I scared you? Ein, what is that?"

"One of Jarl Dagr's guards. He attacked us when we came down to the creek." Ein sat up and looked at him, his little blond eyebrows drawn together in a deep frown. "Don't you remember?"

"Ein, I don't remember anything except coming down to the creek and being attacked. I don't remember what happened after that."

Ein's face blanched. "Nothing?"

"No, wha—" Radulfr suddenly swallowed hard as an image of pure red fury entered his head. "Did I do that?"

Radulfr felt a cold chill run down his spine when Ein nodded. He didn't understand how he could have done that much damage to a human body. The man wasn't simply cut down with a blade. He had been torn apart.

"H–how?"

"He had a sword to my throat. You jumped him and... and... well..."

"Ein!"

"Okay, okay," Ein cried out, "you suddenly grew bigger and you had fur all over your body and these really big teeth. You just kind of attacked him and tore him to shreds with your hands."

Radulfr blinked. Surely he couldn't have heard that right. "I what?"

"You turned into some sort of *Wodan* or something."

Radulfr rolled his eyes. "Don't be ridiculous, Ein. The *Wodan* are a myth. No one magically shifts into a ferocious animal-like creature.

It just doesn't happen. *Wodan* are a battle myth created by people who don't like the fact that they lost the battle."

"Actually, the mythical word is *Wodan*," said a voice from behind Radulfr. "The true word is *Berserkr*."

Radulfr grabbed his sword and swung around in one fluid motion, placing himself between Ein and whatever threat they faced. He held the sword up and slowly waved it back and forth in front of him as he faced a man he had never seen before.

Hell, he hadn't even heard the man walk up.

"Who are you?" Radulfr asked. "What do you want?"

"Calm yourself, Radulfr of Vejle." The man held up his hand in a friendly gesture. "We mean you no harm."

"We?"

Radulfr's unease grew as he glanced around and realized he and Ein were surrounded by three other men—three very large, very naked men. He reached back with one hand and pulled Ein closer to him.

"Who are you?" he asked again.

"I am Baldr." The man bowed his head slightly then waved his hand at the other men. "This is Alimi, Ulfr, and Coinin. We have come to serve you."

Radulfr's mouth dropped open as all four men got down on their knees and bowed their heads at him. Each man pulled their long hair over their shoulders, baring the backs of their necks. He didn't know whether to pat them on the head or strike them down with his sword.

"Radulfr," Ein whispered, "do something."

Radulfr wanted to. He just didn't know what. With no other plan in his mind, Radulfr reached out and gently touched each man on the back of their necks. He inhaled sharply as a flash of white light suddenly filled his head, blinding him for a brief moment. He almost dropped to his knees.

When his vision cleared a moment later, all four men were staring up at him with something akin to pure joy on their faces. It was odd, especially since he could almost feel the elation flowing off of the four men.

"Please, stand up."

The men stood as if they moved as one body. Radulfr and Ein were still surrounded, and he didn't like that very much. He didn't feel unsafe, just cautious. In fact, Radulfr was a little surprised at how safe he did feel.

"Now, who are you and what do you mean you have come to serve me?" Radulfr slowly edged Ein back as he asked his questions. He wanted all four men in front of him, not behind him, just in case.

"We have come to serve you," Baldr said.

"You already said that, but you haven't explained why."

Baldr glanced over at the other three men for a moment then back. Radulfr had the feeling they were somehow communicating with each other. "You are the *drighten*," Baldr said as if Radulfr should have understood that. "As your *thanes*, it is our duty to protect you and your mate."

Radulfr tensed. "My mate?"

"Prophecy says a great warrior will lead our clan to great glory, but he will only come to us once he has taken the *álfar* as his mate." Baldr gestured toward Ein. "This has been done. We've watched you from the woods. We've seen how you protected your mate. We know you are the one."

"When the gods told us of your coming, we could barely believe it," Alimi said. He clasped his hand together in front of him and rocked on the heels of his feet as if he could hardly stand still. "We have waited many years for your arrival."

"What prophecy?" Radulfr asked. "And how do you know I'm the one you've been waiting for?"

"You do not know?" Baldr asked.

Radulfr shook his head.

"But you are the *drighten*," Alimi protested.

"So you've said."

"You shifted," Alimi said. "We saw you shift. You protected your mate, your Elvin mate. It is all part of the prophecy, all signs of your coming."

Radulfr stiffened. "My what?"

He turned slowly to look at Ein. The man was biting his lip. His eyes were downcast, peeking up at him every few seconds then glancing away quickly. He looked guilty as hell. Radulfr suddenly knew the men were correct.

He reached over and grabbed Ein's chin, forcing his head up. "Is there something you forgot to tell me, Ein?"

"I don't know what you mean."

"Ein."

"I'm not supposed to tell you," Ein whispered. His eyes started to fill with tears.

"What weren't you supposed to tell me?"

Ein bit his lip again. His hand trembled when he reached up to tuck his hair behind his ears—his very pointy ears. Radulfr drew in a deep breath as he stared. He remembered those ears. He just didn't remember them being so pointy. He thought his hand might have trembled a little as well as he reached out to gently stroke the curve of Ein's ear.

"You're an *álfar*?"

"Half elf." Ein shrugged. "My *móðir* was human."

"Why didn't you tell me?"

"I can't say."

"Ein!"

"Please." Ein pulled away, his eyes watering even more until two large fat tears trickled down his cheeks. "I can't tell you."

Radulfr heard movement behind him. He tensed and turned, breathing a sigh of relief when he saw the four men had just moved off, giving him and Ein a little space to talk. And talk they would. Radulfr refused to have secrets between them.

He grabbed Ein's arm and led him a few more steps away from the other four men then turned so that he could keep an eye on them. Ein's face was pale as mountaintop snow as Radulfr looked down at him.

"I want the truth, Ein, and I want it now." Radulfr gave Ein a little shake when he started to move his head back and forth. "Ein!"

"I can't."

Radulfr grit his teeth. He grabbed Ein's hand and held it up, gesturing to the ring around his finger. "Do you remember this?" he growled. "This means you owe your allegiance to me and no one else."

Ein's shoulders slumped as he eyed the ring around his finger. "Do you remember that old man I told you about, the one that told me you were coming to claim me?"

"Yes."

"He told me I wasn't supposed to tell you that I was half Elvin."

Radulfr's lips twisted together as he tried to control his anger. He really hated it when other people messed in his life. He got enough of that from the gods. He didn't need it from his mate or a complete stranger.

"If you want to be honest, Ein, you didn't tell me anything. Baldr did."

Ein's head snapped up. A slow smile began to move across his lips. It ripped away Radulfr's anger so fast that he almost staggered under the shock. No one had ever affected him the way Ein did.

"I didn't think of that," Ein whispered.

"What else did the old man tell you?"

Ein's eyes widened and the smile fell off his face. "I… err…"

"You need to tell me, Ein."

Ein sighed deeply. "He said that the path before me wouldn't be an easy one but it would be rewarding, that you would take good care of me once you got over your initial shock. He said you were an honorable man."

"Anything else?"

"He said that you needed someone like me to stand by your side as you rose to power and that you had been chosen by the gods for great things. I just needed to hold out until then."

Radulfr titled his head slightly in confusion. "Why would you need to hold out until then?"

"I am only yours by peace-pledge. There will be those that will not hold me in a good light, but there will be even more that will come to care for me a great deal." Ein swallowed hard and his eyes dropped away from Radulfr's to stare at the ring on his finger again. "Especially you."

Radulfr snarled at Ein's words and dragged him closer. White hot rage filled him. "Peace-pledge or not, you are mine. Don't ever forget that. You belong to me!"

Radulfr didn't know what came over him. Maybe it was the thought that Ein was his only by peace-pledge. Maybe it was the need he felt to claim what was his. Whatever it was, it consumed him until Radulfr growled and sank his teeth in to the soft curve of Ein's neck.

As the sweetest ambrosia he had ever tasted flowed across his tongue, Radulfr heard wolf howls fill the air around him. He drank deeper, harder. He plastered his body against Ein's and swallowed until he heard Ein cry out then slump against him.

The scent of Ein's seed filled the air, mixing with the man's natural fragrance. The combination was overwhelming, arousing Radulfr to staggering heights. His skin suddenly burned. It felt too tight.

Pleasure zipped through him, hitting ever nerve in his body until it exploded in his cock. He pulled his mouth away from Ein's neck and tossed his head back, howling loudly as an intense orgasm suddenly racked his body and took him to his knees.

He cradled Ein to his chest and panted heavily as the pleasure wound down until he could finally breathe again. He chuckled softly, shocked that he had just had an orgasm from biting Ein in the neck.

His shock quickly turned to outright terror when he glanced down at Ein to find him out cold. Ein's head rolled back against his arm when he gave the man a little shake.

"Oh gods, what have I done?" he whispered when his eyes fell on the bleeding wound on Ein's neck. "Ein, *kisa?*"

"Radulfr, if I may?"

Radulfr turned to see Baldr standing beside him. He looked up, agony filling him at the thought that he may have killed his mate. "Please," he begged.

Baldr squatted down and held out a dagger. "You need to drip some of your blood into the bite mark. It will help him heal faster."

"Heal?" Radulfr looked back down at Ein. "He's still alive?"

"He is very much alive, *drighten*. He's just suffering from the first bond bite. His condition is normal."

Radulfr stared at Baldr in horror. "This is normal?"

"Very." Baldr chuckled. "The bond between a *Berserkr* and his mate is sacred. It is also overpowering the first time. It gets easier after this."

"I have to do this again?"

Bader smiled. "You'll want to do this again."

Radulfr took the dagger that Baldr held out to him. He looked at Ein for a moment, unsure of what he should do. "Are you sure about this?"

"I am."

Radulfr hoped Baldr was right. He sliced the dagger across the palm of his hand then dribbled the blood into the bite mark on Ein's neck. The dagger fell from Radulfr's lax fingers, clattering to the ground, as he watched the wound begin to close almost immediately.

"How is this possible?" he whispered.

"A gift from the gods."

* * * *

Radulfr held Ein close to his chest. He felt like he had seen this scene before. A fire had been started, and a rabbit was roasting over the flames. Baldr and Ulfr had gone into the woods and retrieved their horses. They were unloading their gear as Alimi turned the homemade spit over the fire. Coinin stood just outside of the firelight on guard duty.

Radulfr had witnessed scenes like this before, but usually it involved Vidarr and Haakon. He just couldn't figure out why the two men hadn't come to find him before now. The light was setting behind the mountains. He and Ein had been gone for hours. Vidarr and Haakon should have been here before now.

"Baldr, I'm concerned about my men. Ein and I were only to be gone for a small amount of time. They should have come for us by now."

"We saw no men, Radulfr." Baldr waved his hand around the area. "The forest is quiet."

Radulfr tilted his head and listened. Baldr was right. The forest was silent but not in a bad way. He could still hear the creek and the natural sounds of the forest, but other than those made by the people around the campfire, it was like no one else was around for miles.

"Something had to have happened to them," Radulfr said. "Vidarr and Haakon would not leave me of their own free will."

"Do you trust these men?"

"They've had my back for more years than I can remember. I trust them with my life."

Baldr nodded and gestured for Alimi and Ulfr. "Go to the camp on the edge of the forest. See what's going on there. Radulfr's friends are missing, two men named Vidarr and Haakon."

"The tall ones with dark brown hair?" Alimi asked.

Baldr nodded. "They are the ones we saw staying close to Radulfr."

Radulfr stared after Alimi and Ulfr as they ran off then glanced over at Baldr. "Just how long have you been watching me?"

Baldr chuckled. "We picked up your trail outside the *hov* where you retrieved your mate. We've been following you ever since."

"Why?"

Baldr's eyebrow arched. "I thought we already covered that. You are our *drighten*."

"What exactly does that mean?"

Baldr picked up a stick and started drawing circles in the dirt. He seemed to be considering how much to talk about. Radulfr wished he would just tell him everything. He was tired of people meddling in his life and not telling him about it.

"Baldr, I want to know the truth."

"How old do you think I am?" Baldr asked.

"You can't be more than a few winters older than me."

"I've seen one hundred and thirty-seven winters."

"Thor's hammer, that's old."

Baldr let out a bark of laughter. "Thank you."

"You have held up well for one hundred and thirty-seven winters." Radulfr grinned then slowly sobered up as another thought entered his head. "Will I see as many winters?"

"If not more. You are no longer as you were before you entered these woods." Baldr waved the stick around at the trees. "The gods have seen fit to grant you a gift beyond measure."

"What?" Radulfr snapped. "The ability to kill someone with my hands or harm my mate? That doesn't seem like much of a gift to me."

"There is more to being a *Berserkr* than killing, Radulfr."

"Like what?" Radulfr didn't see it. He couldn't stop thinking about the danger he had put Ein in. The bite mark on his neck had closed up, but the man had yet to wake. Radulfr was pretty sure he'd be worried until Ein opened his eyes.

"Lift your nose into the air and take a deep breath," Baldr said. "What do you smell?"

Radulfr frowned but did as Baldr asked. He inhaled deeply and was assaulted with so many scents all at once that his eyes watered. He could smell the trees, the dirt, even the animals moving about. He could smell it all. "By the gods!"

Baldr chuckled. "Yes, that is true. It is only by the gods that we are granted these abilities. Every sense we have has been enhanced—sight, sound, smell, touch, even our sixth sense. We are who we were before, but we are more once we change."

Radulfr remembered the itch he had felt move over his skin, the fury that had filled him when Ein had been attacked, and even the need to taste Ein's blood. It scared him, but it also intrigued him.

"How did this happen?" Radulfr asked. "I mean, how did the *Berserkrs* come about?"

"That, my friend, is a myth." Baldr chuckled. "Legend says that a village was attacked a thousand winters past. The *seið-kona* of this village prayed to the gods for revenge on those that had slaughtered everyone. The gods granted his prayer, but it came with a price."

"I think I can guess what that price was."

"Then I believe you would be surprised."

Radulfr frowned. "Are you telling me that becoming whatever it is we become was not the price?"

"No."

"Then what? Blood drinking?"

"Again, you are wrong, my friend."

Radulfr gave Baldr an exasperated look. Baldr chuckled and nodded to the man sleeping in Radulfr's arms. Radulfr glanced down, unsure of exactly what Baldr was indicating, but as he stared at Ein, he began to suspect that he knew.

"Ein?"

Baldr shrugged. "Or men like him. Because we are battle warriors we are unable to find our mates in the female populace." Baldr waved his hand absently. "Some agreement between Thor, the god of war, and Freyja, the goddess of love. Freyja insisted that even warriors needed mates. Thor insisted that those mates be male so they could stand by our side if need be."

"You all prefer men then?"

"Don't you?"

"I've been with both, but yes, I suppose I do. Men seem to understand me better. I guess I've never really thought about it that much."

"Well, you might want to think about it because I believe your little mate is waking up."

Radulfr looked down at the man in his arms so fast he felt his neck muscles strain. Baldr was correct, though. Ein's eyes were beginning to flutter as if he was waking up. Radulfr heard Baldr get up and walk away but Ein had his complete attention.

"*Kisa*, open your eyes."

Chapter 7

Ein heard Radulfr calling out to him. He blinked several times before he was able to keep his eyes open. He felt Radulfr's hand stroke the side of his face. He smiled and leaned into the gentle touch.

"Radulfr," he whispered.

"How do you feel, *Kisa*?"

"Thirsty."

Radulfr chucked. "Baldr, could you bring my mate some water? He's thirsty."

A water pouch appeared seconds later. Ein drank greedily when Radulfr held the water pouch up to his mouth. He whimpered when it was pulled away.

"Not too much, Ein," Radulfr said. "I don't want you to get sick."

"What happened?"

The last thing he could remember was talking with Radulfr about the things his *grandfaðir* told him. He still hadn't told Radulfr that the old man was his *grandfaðir* or who his *grandfaðir* really was. He really didn't want to have that conversation.

"I bit you."

Ein blinked and tilted his head back. "You did what?"

Radulfr's face flushed. "I bit you."

Ein worried his bottom lip between his teeth. Was there really any response he could say to that that didn't make him seem like a complete fool?

"I'm sorry, Ein," Radulfr said quickly. "I didn't mean to. I just couldn't stop myself. You smelled so good, and once I bit you, you tasted so good. I just couldn't stop. By the time I reached orgasm, you had passed out."

Ein felt like his eyes were going to bug right out of his head. "You had an orgasm from biting me?"

Radulfr's face turned beet red. Ein didn't feel quite the same embarrassment. The idea that he could bring Radulfr enough pleasure from just tasting his blood to make the man orgasm thrilled Ein right down to his toes.

"Do you want to bite me again?"

"Ein!"

Ein laughed. He felt surprisingly wonderful, but he wasn't sure if it came from knowing he had brought Radulfr pleasure or from the abashed look on Radulfr's face, especially since it was tempered with intrigue.

"You can, you know," Ein said as he leaned closer to Radulfr. "I belong to you. You can bite me whenever you desire."

Ein grunted when Radulfr growled and reached for him. He suddenly found himself crushed against Radulfr's chest. Hot, heavy breath blew out across his neck. Ein shuddered when he felt Radulfr's tongue stroke across his skin. Maybe he'd like this whole biting thing as well.

"Are you going to bite me again?" Ein whispered as Radulfr continued to lick at the small bite mark on his neck.

Radulfr groaned and pushed back far enough so he could look into Ein's face. The man seemed agonized—his face was flush and tense. Ein could see a small pulse in Radulfr's clenched jaw. It was actually fascinating to watch.

"You have no idea how much I want to taste you again, Ein." Radulfr's voice was rough, low, and gravelly. He nodded his head toward the men standing on the other side of the roaring fire. "However, considering what happened the last time I bit you, now may not be the right time to do so again."

Ein glanced over. Baldr and Coinin looked like their attention was engaged elsewhere, but he could see the sly little looks the two men kept aiming his way. Radulfr was right. Now was not the time or the place.

Ein didn't mind Radulfr biting him again. In fact, he looked forward to it. But having their intimate moments together watched already didn't mean he wanted it to happen again. He'd prefer a little privacy.

Ein leaned up and whispered in Radulfr's ear, "Later we can find time alone, yes?"

Radulfr chuckled and tightened his arms around Ein. "I would not have it any other way, *kisa*."

Ein cocked his head to the side. "*Kisa*... why do you keep calling me a kitten? I may be smaller than you, but I'm still a man."

Radulfr chuckled. "You are, and I thank the gods for this. But I call you *kisa* because you love to be touched and caressed. You mewl when I touch you and you curl into me like a small kitten. That makes you my *kisa*."

Ein's face flushed horribly, but he couldn't help but lean into the hand Radulfr held against his cheek. Radulfr was correct. He did love to be touched and caressed. He craved it almost more than his next breath. If Radulfr wanted to call him *kisa* because of it, he'd deal with it.

"If that is your wish," Ein said.

"It is."

Ein laughed and burrowed into the crook of Radulfr's neck. The man could call him anything he wanted as long as he never stopped wanting him. Ein didn't know what he would do if Radulfr stopped wanting him—die of a broken heart probably.

"Here."

Ein turned his head, refusing to move away from his comfortable spot cuddled against Radulfr. Baldr was squatted next to them, holding out some meat. Ein snatched it away and started chewing, suddenly realizing he was starving.

He groaned as the smoky taste of the roasted rabbit hit his stomach. He wasn't a huge fan of rabbit, but as hungry as he was, it tasted like the ambrosia of the gods. "This is delicious."

Baldr chuckled. "Glad you think so, little one."

Ein frowned up at the large man as he ate. "Who are you?"

"As I have explained to Radulfr, we are here to serve him, just as you do."

Ein blinked and paused, a strip of rabbit meat halfway to his mouth. "I serve him?"

"Do you not?" Baldr asked. "Radulfr is *drighten*. We all serve him one manner or another."

Ein frowned over at Radulfr when a bark of laughter fell from the man's lips. "This amuses you?"

Radulfr waved his hands frantically, but Ein wasn't fooled by his innocent gesture. The laughter alone told him that Radulfr found the whole situation vastly entertaining. The corners of Ein's lips began to pull up despite his disgruntlement.

The light-hearted contentment coming from Radulfr pulled away Ein's anger and replaced it with a tranquility of its own. Ein found that he couldn't be upset with Radulfr, not when faced with the man's happiness.

Baldr was a different matter. Ein didn't owe the man his allegiance. Ein curled his lips back down and turned his anger on him. The smile instantly fell from Baldr's face when he looked at Ein.

"Uh…"

"Yes?" Ein asked, arching his eyebrow. "You have something to say?"

"No, not a word."

Ein blinked when Baldr suddenly jumped to his feet and raced across the campground to start gathering firewood from the edge of the tree line. Radulfr's chest rumbled against Ein's side as the man threw back his head and let out a great peal of laughter.

"You, *kisa*, are an amazing man."

"Me?"

"How big do you think Baldr is?"

Ein glanced over at the large man. He shrugged. "I do not know. He seems nearly as big as you."

"He's bigger," Radulfr said. "Baldr actually stands a little taller than I do. I also imagine he weighs several stone more than me. He is a very large man."

"And?"

"And, you, my sexy little *kisa*, just scared him across the camp."

"I did no such thing."

Radulfr roared with laughter again. Ein felt his face flush as he dipped his head. He peeked out at Baldr through his bangs. Surely the large man couldn't be afraid of him. Baldr could crush him with a single blow.

"I am *drighten*, Ein, and you are my mate, the most important person in my world," Radulfr said when he finally stopped laughing. "That makes you a very powerful man indeed."

Ein suddenly didn't care if he scared Baldr. Just hearing Radulfr's words was enough to make him shout with delight inside. He smiled and shoved his embarrassment away as he snuggled into Radulfr's arms.

"I can live with that."

"Oh, you do please me, *kisa*. You please me greatly." Ein felt Radulfr's lips press against his forehead. "I was blessed by the gods the day I sealed our *hansal* with a hand-clasp. Jarl Dagr would be berating himself if he knew what he had lost."

Ein beamed. He prayed to the gods that Jarl Dagr never learned of his mistake. Ein was perfectly happy right where he was.

A loud crash suddenly came from the other side of the camp. Ein felt Radulfr's arms tighten around him as they both looked up to see several men break through the tree line. Ein immediately recognized Vidarr and Haakon, plus the other two strangers from before.

They all looked dirty and tired. Vidarr and Haakon seemed even worse. Several places on their clothing had been ripped away or torn. Bruises darkened their faces. Vidarr had dried blood on his forehead.

Ein stood as Radulfr jumped to his feet. Anxiety started to fill him then run rampant. He twisted his hands together and watched Radulfr hurry over to his friends. Something horrible had obviously happened to the two men. Ein was almost afraid to ask.

Radulfr, apparently, wasn't. He grabbed Vidarr by his arm as the man slowly sank down to the ground, Haakon sitting right behind him.

"What's going on? What happened?"

"Glad to see you safe, old friend," Vidarr said. "We were unsure if you had been captured or not."

"We were attacked," Radulfr said, "but—"

"Jarl Dagr's men?" Vidarr asked.

"Yes."

Vidarr nodded. "You were not the only one. Someone knocked me over the head. When I came to, Haakon and I were both tied up. The lawspeaker's guards are dead. Jarl Dagr's men were not alone. They had friends."

Radulfr squatted down next to Vidarr. "Are you sure it was Jarl Dagr's men?"

Vidarr shrugged. "They seemed to know each other."

"They were a might friendly," Haakon added. "They took great pleasure in roughing us up together."

"Are you okay?" Ein asked. He didn't know Haakon and Vidarr that well, but he had come to greatly like the men in the last several days. He ached to think they had been harmed.

Haakon smiled at him from across the camp. "We are good, little one. Thank you for asking."

"*Drighten*," Baldr said as he stepped up to Radulfr, "we must go. Alimi said more men are coming. We are no longer safe here."

Radulfr nodded and stood. Ein's heart thundered in his chest as he ran across the camp to stand next to Radulfr. His hands wouldn't stop shaking. Even when Radulfr's arm wrapped around him, Ein couldn't stop thinking about what might happen to them all if they got caught. It terrified him.

"Radulfr?" Ein couldn't keep the worry out of his voice.

"Not to worry, Ein," Baldr said. "Our duty to Radulfr includes keeping you both safe from harm. We will not let these men have you."

"Duty? *Drighten*?" Vidarr asked. "Of what does he speak, Radulfr?"

"It is a tale we do not have time for me to tell, my friend. I believe we need to leave," Radulfr replied. "Baldr, do we have enough horses to carry us all?"

"If a few of us double up, we should be fine."

Radulfr nodded. When he turned and gestured, Ein stepped closer. "Are you ready to ride, *kisa*?"

Ein nodded. He really had no idea what he was ready for beyond not staying if it meant more soldiers were coming. If Radulfr wanted him to ride, he'd ride. "Can I ride with you?"

"I would not have it any other way, Ein."

Everything after that kind of happened rather quickly for Ein. He stood there and watched everyone hurry about the campsite. The fire was extinguished, the rabbit wrapped up for later. The horses were readied for riding and all the gear reloaded.

Ein stood there feeling totally useless as everyone moved around him. He didn't know anything about riding horses, let alone getting them ready to ride. The horses at the *hov* were used for field work, not riding.

"Come, *kisa*. It's time to go."

Ein ran over to where Radulfr stood next to a large black horse. The animal stood nearly as tall as him. Ein swallowed past the fear building in his throat. He couldn't tear his eyes away from the large horse.

"Uh, Radulfr, I'm not sure I can ride this thing. Maybe we can go back and get my horse?" He liked the horse Radulfr brought him to ride. She was smaller, gentler.

"Calm yourself, Ein."

Ein yelped when Radulfr suddenly picked him up and tossed him onto the back of the horse. He was so far up he felt like he was standing on top of the roof of the *byre*. Radulfr grabbed the horse's mane and pulled himself up behind him. Ein instantly wiggled back until he sat huddled in the curve of Radulfr's body.

"Ready, *kisa*?"

"What if I say no?"

Radulfr chuckled. "Not a choice, little one. If we want to live to see another dawn, we need to escape whoever is chasing us."

"Then I suppose I am ready."

Ein knew he lied through his teeth the moment Radulfr snapped the reins and the horse shot forward. His heart jumped into his throat, and he scrambled to grab on to anything to keep himself from falling off the horse. Radulfr's arms tightened around him.

"Easy, *kisa*," he whispered against the side of Ein's head. "I won't let you fall."

"This seemed so much easier on the other horse."

"It was. You have to remember, Ein, I was coming to claim my bride. I brought a horse fit for a lady to ride, not a man."

"I'm not a lady," Ein snorted.

"And thank the gods for that." Radulfr chuckled. "I much prefer you this way."

Ein blinked, not sure how to reply to that. He still worried that Radulfr would suddenly wake up one day and decide he didn't want to be peace-pledged to a man. He'd been waiting for that to happen since the moment he met the man. To hear Radulfr say he preferred him as a man was surprising.

"You are the jarl of your clan," Ein said. "You know it will not be easy when you bring me home. Besides me being a man, there is still the whole peace-pledge thing to deal with. People won't accept this easily."

"It matters not, Ein. I am jarl and I accept you. That will be enough for my clan."

Ein had serious doubts about that. He understood that Radulfr was the leader of his clan, but he also knew people. They might look the other way to a little man-on-man indiscretion, but they would never accept Radulfr and him being together long-term. He just hoped Radulfr didn't come to hate him when the time came.

"Hold on, Ein," Radulfr said as his arms tightened. "It's rough riding from here on out."

Ein held on for dear life.

Chapter 8

Radulfr rubbed his cheek along the top of Ein's head. They had been riding for hours. Dawn had long ago risen, and now the sun was starting to set, darkness coming. His little mate was sound asleep, snuggled deeply into his arms. He had been sleeping on and off for most of the day.

Radulfr worried about the stress their travels might have on Ein. As far as he knew, Ein spent his entire life at the *hov*. He wasn't prepared for long travel. He certainly wasn't prepared for them to be running for their lives.

If Ein had not been with him, Radulfr would have stayed and fought. He detested running. But putting Ein in danger wasn't an option. If he needed to run with his tail between his legs to keep his mate safe, he'd do it.

"*Drighten*, your mate is okay?"

Radulfr smiled over at Alimi. "He is only sleeping. Ein is not used to these long travels. I think all of the stress has gotten to him."

"Would you like me to take him for a while?"

Radulfr's arms tightened around Ein. A small growl escaped his lips. "I'll keep him."

Alimi smiled and nodded. "As you wish, *drighten*."

"Radulfr. My name is Radulfr."

Alimi nodded again.

Radulfr rolled his eyes and went back to looking ahead. He wasn't sure he believed that he was this mythical *drighten* that Alimi and his friends believed he was. He was still having trouble believing he transformed into some mythical beast.

"Your friends, they are okay?"

"What?" Radulfr swung around to look at Alimi again. The man was looking ahead of them to where Vidarr and Haakon rode with Baldr and Ulfr. "Oh, yes, I believe they are. Nothing a warm bed and a hot meal won't cure."

"You've known them long?"

Radulfr frowned at the curiosity he could hear in Alimi's voice. He followed the trail of the man's gaze then bit back a smile when he figured out who held Alimi's interest. Life was getting more interesting by the moment, and not just for him.

"I've known Vidarr and Haakon most of my life."

Alimi glanced over at him. The tenseness of the man's jaw told Radulfr he wanted to ask more, but he was either embarrassed to or afraid to. Radulfr wasn't sure which. He could, however, satisfy some of Alimi's curiosity.

"We all grew up in the same small town. Haakon was fostered with me at an early age. His parents were killed in a raid. Vidarr was fostered with me a couple of years later when his family moved to our clan."

"They are good men?"

"The best a man could ask for," Radulfr replied. "We've fought many battles together. They've had my back more times than I can count. I'd even trust them with Ein."

"High praise."

"They have earned it. They are honorable men. They have proven themselves on the field of battle and even off of it. I trust no one more." Radulfr knew Alimi understood his meaning when the man nodded. "I can only hope that their loyalty is rewarded one day and they find their own mates."

Radulfr chuckled when Alimi almost fell off his horse. The man was see-through. His interest in Vidarr and Haakon was so apparent, it was almost tangible. Radulfr didn't know hardly anything about

Alimi, but if mating with him could bring his friends happiness, Radulfr was all for it.

"Vidarr's life hadn't been a happy one. He may have grown up with parents when Haakon didn't, but Vidarr's parents could barely be called that. They were far more concerned with their *sonr* marrying into the right family than they were with Vidarr being happy."

"They would disapprove of him mating with a man?"

"They certainly wouldn't be in support of it," Radulfr snorted. "It wouldn't be acceptable to them. They harp on Vidarr every time they see him about his dalliances with other men. It's gotten to the point that Vidarr avoids his parents whenever he can just so he doesn't have to hear it."

"Damn."

Radulfr couldn't agree more. He knew his *faðir* wasn't thrilled that he preferred men, but he kept quiet about it since Radulfr was the jarl. His mother passed to the gods long before Radulfr even knew he preferred men.

"Haakon's story is altogether different. His parents were killed in a raid when he was a young child. His *móðir* was distantly related to my *faðir*, so Haakon was brought to my clan and raised there."

"That doesn't sound so bad."

"Maybe, but I think Haakon has always felt a little on the outside of things being raised with no parents. There are those in the clan that never let him forget he was fostered with me because he didn't have a family of his own."

"I understand how he feels. Coinin, my brother, and I were banished, considered *warg* when it was discovered we were *Berserkrs*." Alimi spit on the ground then grimaced. "Our own parents were with the mob that drove us from our home."

"But..." Radulfr's jaw dropped as he fought for words. "Being a *Berserkr* is not a crime. You can only become *warg* if you've committed a crime."

Alimi shrugged. "We were no longer considered human."

"That's ridiculous," Radulfr snapped. The very idea that Alimi and Coinin, as well as the others, might not be considered human because of their ability to transform rankled Radulfr. It was wrong. "If Baldr was correct in what he told me, this ability comes from the gods themselves. That means we are blessed by the gods, not a *geas*."

"I agree, *drighten*, but not everyone does. Many see us as a curse. They are afraid of us and what we can do. They say we are a threat to our own people, that we kill and maim indiscriminately. They shun us."

"How do you live? Survive?"

"We keep mostly to ourselves." Alimi chuckled. "Baldr has a farm on the outreaches of a river. We stay there often, but mostly we roam the countryside. We've spent years searching for you, and that has taken us in many different directions."

Radulfr was slightly surprised by the amusement in Alimi's face when the man looked over at him. Considering the subject matter of their conversation, he couldn't think of a single thing that would be amusing.

"We also spend much of our time in our wolf form, roaming the woods. You wouldn't believe how many people avoid the woods when they think there is a band of vicious wolves living in them."

Radulfr chuckled. The mental image alone made him see what Alimi found so funny. Still… "As grand as that sounds, I'd appreciate if you didn't try and scare anyone off when we get home. My people will need time to adjust to this."

"Do you really believe they will, *drighten*?"

Radulfr frowned. "Why wouldn't they?"

"Our world is not an easy one, despite being blessed by the gods. So many are afraid of us. They do not understand the gift we have been given. Most would rather slay us than ask questions."

There was a hint of sadness in Alimi's eyes and Radulfr knew no matter how much the man might pretend otherwise, the shunning from his parents and clan still weighed heavy on him.

"Alimi, has it ever been explained why we've been gifted by the gods?" Radulfr asked. "What is the purpose of this gift? And why did the gods choose us?"

"We protect those that cannot protect themselves."

Radulfr waited for Alimi to say more. He didn't. "And? Why did they gods choose us?"

Alimi smiled. "That I cannot say. Each of us are chosen for different reasons."

"Why were you chosen?"

"I'm very fast, faster than even Baldr. Each of us brings something to the group. Ulfr, as you can guess from his size, brings strength. Baldr brings cunning, and Coinin is the most resourceful man I know."

"And me, why have I been chosen?"

"You've been chosen to lead us."

Radulfr rolled his eyes. "The gods must be crazy."

Before Alimi could say more, Baldr rode back to them. "We've ridden for many hours. The horses need to rest or they will be useless to us. I suspect the rest of us could use some rest as well. I suggest we stop at the bottom of that hill just ahead."

Radulfr nodded. He knew he could use a rest, and he imagined Ein needed to stretch his legs as well. "We'll need to have a cold camp. Any fire could be seen for miles. Do we have enough supplies?"

"We still have some roasted rabbit, *drighten*," Baldr said, "and I believe that Ulfr has some dried fish. That and some flatbread should fill us sufficiently until we can trade for more supplies."

"Is there enough water for Ein to wash?" Radulfr asked. "He really dislikes being dirty."

Baldr smiled as he looked at the man sleeping in Radulfr's arms. "I'm sure we can arrange something. There is a small brook just a little past the bottom of the hill. If we ride to there, Ein wouldn't have to leave camp to wash."

Radulfr was in full support of that idea. He remembered what happened the last time they went to wash. It was one of the reasons they were in this mess. Still, he wanted to make things as normal as possible for Ein, even if it meant riding a little longer so they could reach fresh water.

"I'd prefer that we rode on so Ein can have the use of the brook. He is unused to being in danger. We need to reassure him and make him feel safe."

"If I may make a suggestion, *drighten*?" Baldr asked.

Radulfr nodded.

"As much as we can try and keep things calm for your mate, telling him of the danger we are in might be a better choice. He needs to know. Not telling him could bring him even more danger."

Radulfr shook his head. "Ein has lived his entire life in the *hov*. He does not know of the dangers out here in the real world. As much as I wish for him to accept life out here, I do not know if he will be as he is now if he knows he is in constant danger."

"Telling him of the danger is not the same as changing his innocence, *drighten*. We can still keep him safe, but if he knows of the danger, he will be better prepared when it occurs." Baldr grimaced. "And you now it will occur. We do not live a life of peace."

"I just want…" Radulfr pressed his lips together as he gazed down into Ein's sweet face. The man was so innocent, so naive about the real world. Radulfr didn't want that innocent torn away from Ein. It was part of what made Ein so special. "I don't want him to be afraid," he finally whispered.

"Then teach him to defend himself," Baldr said sternly. "Give him the power to protect himself. Make sure that when danger does come, Ein has the skills to stand by your side."

"I don't want him to stand by my side!" Radulfr snapped.

"Then where do you want him to stand?" Baldr barked right back. "Behind you?"

"No, but—"

Radulfr wanted to growl at Baldr, to shout at him. The man didn't understand. Ein was special. He was sweet and kind, and he couldn't hurt a soul. The gods would be cruel indeed to take that away from Ein, to take it away from Radulfr.

Radulfr grabbed the reins in one hand and rubbed the bridge of his nose with the other. He wished he could put into words how much Ein's sweet nature affected him, but doing so would admit a weakness, and Radulfr wasn't sure he was ready for that.

He hadn't admitted to a weakness since he was ten years old and his mother passed away. His *faðir* had caught him crying over her grave the day after she was buried and beat him within an inch of his life. He never showed vulnerability again.

Not until Ein.

"We'll warn him to stay close to us and teach him how defend himself with a dagger," Radulfr said. "But I don't want his love for life taken from him. His safety and well-being is to take precedence over everything else."

"As you wish, *drighten*."

Radulfr thought Baldr might have been placating him, but when he glanced at the man, Baldr was grinning. "You have something to add, Baldr?"

"You care for him a great deal, do you not?"

A tender smile crossed Radulfr's lips as he gently rubbed the side of Ein's face. "He's special. I doubt there is anyone like him on earth."

"I am sure you are correct, *drighten*."

Radulfr sent Baldr a little glare until the man rode off, laughing. He knew he was right. Ein was special. Radulfr had no idea why he had been blessed with the man's care, but he swore to himself he would never forsake the gods that gave Ein to him. He'd spend the rest of his life trying to make Ein happy and keep him safe.

"*Drighten*, may I ask a question?"

"Of course, Alimi."

"Why have you chosen to teach Ein how to handle a dagger? Why not your sword?"

"Ein and a sword?" Radulfr laughed. "He's not strong enough to even lift my sword, let alone wield it."

"I do not understand." Alimi started to frown. "He was holding your sword just fine when we came upon him. He seemed to have no trouble handling it."

"Ein was wielding my sword?" Radulfr gasped.

He couldn't even imagine Ein holding his sword much less using it. His sword was huge, heavy. It had been specially made just for him as a present from Vidarr and Haakon when he became jarl. Even Vidarr, as big as he was, had a hard time wielding it.

"He was." Alimi chuckled. "He stood right over the top of you swinging that sword back and forth as we walked up. He had every intention on protecting you from harm. And, if you don't mind my saying so, *drighten*, he was doing a pretty damn good job of it."

Radulfr was shocked, not only that Ein had used his sword but that the man had tried to protect him when he couldn't protect himself. It spoke a lot toward Ein's personality and the future of their relationship. If Ein cared enough to try and protect him, they might have more in common that Radulfr thought.

"We're here, Radulfr."

Radulfr glanced up and saw the men ahead of them climbing off their horses. He pulled his own horse to a stop and waited for Baldr to walk over. Radulfr handed Ein down to Baldr, climbed off his own horse, then quickly took Ein back into his arms. Ein never woke.

"He may not make it to the brook." Baldr chuckled.

"He's not used to riding all day long."

"I imagine not." Baldr handed off the reins of the horse to Alimi then turned back toward Radulfr. "I'll get a bed roll out for him if you wish. He can always use the brook in the morning before we head out."

Radulfr nodded. "That sounds good, thank you, Baldr, but I think he needs to eat something first. He needs to keep up his strength."

"Then I'll get things unpacked if you want to wake him."

Radulfr nodded and carried Ein over to a fallen log. He sat down and cradled Ein in his arms then started gently stroking his hand over the side of the man's face. Ein's eyes began to flutter.

"Hey, *kisa*," Radulfr said softly when the man finally opened his eyes all of the way. "Did you sleep well?"

Ein sat up and pushed his hair back from his face as he looked around. "Where are we?"

"We've stopped to eat and let the horses get some rest."

"Are we safe here?"

"You, little one, are safe wherever we are." Radulfr pointed to the other men around the small clearing. "I've made it clear to everyone that your safety comes before anything else. If something happens and you can't get to me, go to one of them. They will protect you with their lives."

"What?" Ein swung around. "No, I don't—"

Radulfr pressed his finger against Ein's lips, quieting him. "It's not up to you to decide. It's up to me, and I say you stay safe no matter what. Your safety is more important than anything."

Radulfr pulled a small sheathed dagger out of his belt and handed it to Ein. It was the same one he had been whittling with back at the creek. "This is for you. I want you to keep it on you at all times. Vidarr and I will teach you a few moves with it, enough to wield it safely and effectively."

Ein's hand trembled as he reached over to take the dagger. He held it cautiously on his hand, trailing his fingers over the faded leather sheath. His eyebrows were drawn together as if he were confused and trying to figure something out.

"What, Ein?"

"Are we in that much danger still?" he asked in a low voice. "I thought that was what this riding was all about, getting away from whoever attacked us. Haven't we done that?"

Radulfr sighed. "I cannot say, *kisa*. We haven't seen a sign of whoever is after us for some hours, but that does not mean they aren't still after us. Our biggest worry is when we get home. If they are indeed Jarl Dagr's men, then they know where we live."

Ein's face turned pale white, just the reaction Radulfr was hoping to avoid. He damned Baldr to the depths of hell as he drew Ein back to his chest. So much for the man's idea of telling Ein the truth. Ein was terrified.

"Hey." Radulfr grabbed Ein's chin and tilted it up. "From what I hear from Baldr and Alimi, you're already pretty good at protecting yourself, me as well. Although, how you even lifted my sword let alone wielded it is beyond me. The thing must be as nearly as big as you."

Sunlight blond hair fell over Ein's forehead as he tilted his head slightly. "But it wasn't, not really. I didn't think I'd be able to lift it at all, but I did. It didn't feel that heavy at all."

The idea that Ein could use his sword intrigued Radulfr more than he could say. He set Ein on his feet then drew his sword from the scabbard at his waist. He lifted it up and held the long sword out to Ein.

"Here, take it. Show me."

Ein rolled his eyes and reached over, grabbing the sword by the hilt with both hands. Silence fell over the small campsite as Ein effortlessly lifted the sword into the air and swung it around like an expert.

"What do you want me to do with it?"

Radulfr blinked. He was in shock. He couldn't utter a word. Ein looked like he had handled a sword since before he could walk. He was swinging it through the air like it was the most natural thing in the world.

"Just swing it around a little, Ein," Baldr said. "We want to see what you can do with it."

Radulfr felt the man come up and stop next to him. A moment later, Vidarr and Haakon walked up, followed quickly by Alimi, Coinin, and Ulfr until Ein was surrounded by all of them. Radulfr could see the surprise and shock on their faces. They were all fascinated by Ein's skill in wielding the sword.

"What else can you do with it, Ein?" Radulfr asked. "Do you know how to wield a blade during a sword fight?"

The sword dipped down toward the ground. "No, I've never held a sword before now. They weren't allowed in the *hov*," Ein replied. "But you can teach me."

Radulfr chuckled at the eager look on Ein's face. He held out his hand. If he was going to teach Ein how to handle a word, he preferred to use his own sword. "Does anyone have a spare sword that Ein can use?"

"He may use mine," Vidarr said as he withdrew the large blade from the scabbard at his waist.

"Ein, hand me my sword just the way I handed it to you."

Ein listened well, holding the sword out with both hands. Radulfr felt pride race through him when he took the sword and placed it back into the scabbard. Maybe it wouldn't be so hard to teach him a few moves.

"Now, carefully take Vidarr's sword just the way you took mine."

Vidarr held out the sword. Ein reached for it. The smile fell from his lips as the sword clattered to the ground. His mouth dropped open as he stared up at Vidarr.

"I am so sorry," he said.

Ein reached down to grab the sword. His fingers wrapped around the hilt. He grunted as he lifted it up. It was obvious to Radulfr that he struggled to pick the sword up. Ein needed to grab it with both hands just to get the hilt off the ground.

"Ein, wait."

Ein's face was tense as he looked up. "I didn't mean to drop it. It's just so heavy."

Radulfr's eyebrows shot up. "It's heavy?"

Ein nodded. "It's much heavier than yours. Is it made of some other type of metal?"

"Uh, Ein, my sword is made of the same metal as Vidarr's."

"Then why is it so heavy?" Ein's tongue came out to rub against the edge of his lower lip as he tried to lift the sword in the air. He panted, huffed and puffed, then finally sighed deeply as he let the sword tip sink back to the ground. "It's just too heavy, Radulfr. I can't lift it. I'd rather use yours."

Radulfr chuckled as he reached over and took the sword from Ein and handed it back to Vidarr. He pulled his out and held it up to Ein. Something cold shivered down his spine when Ein took it with ease, handling the sword like it weighed no more than the dagger he had given him earlier.

"That is incredibly strange, Radulfr," Vidarr said.

Radulfr nodded.

"You all are playing a joke on me, aren't you?" Ein laughed as he swung the sword effortlessly in the air. "Radulfr's sword isn't made of the same stuff. It can't be."

"I promise, *kisa*, my sword is made of the same metal as Vidarr's."

"But how?" Ein's eyebrows drew together. He slowly lowered the tip of the sword toward the ground. "How is this possible?"

"A gift from the gods," Baldr said.

Radulfr rolled his eyes. "That's your answer for everything, Baldr. It doesn't explain how Ein can wield my sword and not Vidarr's."

"Actually, I believe it does." Baldr rubbed his chin as he watched Ein. "Let's try something, huh?"

"Nothing that will hurt Ein," Radulfr growled.

"No, no." Baldr waved a hand dismissively at Radulfr. "I just want to try something."

"What?"

"Ein, give the sword back to Radulfr and get out the dagger he gave you a few minutes ago."

Ein looked confused but did as Baldr asked. Radulfr felt just as confused as Ein when Baldr took the dagger away from Ein and held it out to him.

"Show me what you can do with this," Baldr said, "and I want you to really show us everything. Consider it a form of bragging. You want Ein to see everything that can be done with a dagger."

Radulfr had no idea where Baldr was going with his little theory, but considering how strange things were at the moment, he was willing to give the man a chance. He took the dagger from Ein and began putting on a performance.

He twirled the dagger, tossed it into the air, and caught it. He spun the tip on the end of his finger. And then Radulfr started throwing the dagger at targets—first a tree, then a stump. He even threw the dagger at a piece of wood that Vidarr held up for him. He put on the performance of his life.

Finally, Radulfr was out of things to do with the dagger. He tossed it up into the air one last time then handed it back to Ein when he was done. He turned to Baldr and arched an eyebrow.

"Was that what you wanted?"

"Very impressive, *drighten*." Baldr turned to Ein and nodded at the knife. "Now you do it, exactly as Radulfr did."

Radulfr sat down heavily on the fallen log when his legs suddenly didn't want to hold him up anymore. He couldn't believe what he was watching. It had to be some sort of magic. Ein was doing exactly what he had done, almost as if it was Radulfr was doing it.

"I don't understand how this is possible," he whispered as Ein stuck the dagger back into the sheath he had given him.

"I've told you, *drighten*, it's a gift from the gods."

Radulfr's nostrils flared as he glared up at Baldr. "Ein can handle a dagger just as well as I can, and I know he's never handled one in his life. He can also wield my sword, but only my sword. How is that a gift from the gods?"

"Ein's ability to handle a dagger and your sword alone isn't the gift. Ein himself is the gift from the gods, *drighten*, a gift to you."

Chapter 9

Ein chewed the cold rabbit meat carefully and slowly. He knew there was not that much to go around, no matter what the others said or how much they offered him. He wanted to be sure everyone got their fair share. The slower he chewed, the more there would be for everyone. Still, he eagerly took the piece of flatbread that Radulfr handed him and ate it.

Ein was a little surprised by how accepted he felt by the larger warriors. They included him in conversation and never once made him feel like he was less than them because he wasn't a warrior.

He leaned back farther into the apex of Radulfr's thighs and smiled as he listened to Haakon tell some tall tale of bravery and courage in battle. It was a fascinating tale that held Ein's interest until he felt Radulfr's arms close around him, and then Ein forgot all about what Haakon was saying.

Ein sat on the ground between Radulfr's legs. Radulfr sat on a log behind him. Ein glanced up curiously when Radulfr slid down and rested against the fallen log. When Radulfr pulled back on his shoulders, Ein leaned back against him.

Ein's eyes widened when Radulfr draped his heavy fur cloak over the both of them. He quickly dropped his eyes so no one could see his shock when Radulfr's hands began to roam over his chest. He leaned his head back against Radulfr's chest and tilted his head up.

"What are you doing?" he murmured.

"Enjoying the gift the gods have given me, what else?"

"We're not alone."

"We're under my cloak. As long as you don't make any noises, they will never know."

Ein wondered how in the hell he was supposed to keep quiet when Radulfr's hands were pushing under his shirt and moving along his sensitive skin. It would be nearly impossible. It felt too good.

"Radulfr," Ein moaned.

Radulfr's hands had moved up Ein's chest to play with his nipples. It was incredibly hot. Ein could feel his cock hardening until he ached. His head pressed back against Radulfr harder and harder as his nipples were tugged, twisted, and made to throb.

"You are so responsive, *kisa*."

Ein inhaled swiftly when Radulfr's hands started moving down his chest. Every little stroke of the man's fingers felt so good against his skin. He felt like his entire body was wired directly to Radulfr.

Ein had no idea when he talked to his *grandfaðir* that he would find such pleasure in Radulfr's arms. Each touch was magical. Ein felt like Radulfr was his gift from the gods, not the other way around.

When Radulfr's hands started to untie his pants, Ein's gaze flew to the other men sitting around the small camp. He breathed a sigh of relief when no one seemed to be looking at them or even paying them any attention. Conversation was going on like something earth-shattering wasn't happening just a few feet away.

"Radulfr, we can't," Ein whispered even as spread his legs. He could have no more prevented himself from moving up into Radulfr's firm touch than he could have stopped breathing.

"Yes, *kisa*," Radulfr said as his fingers closed around Ein's hard, leaking cock, "we can."

Ein bit his lip when he groaned, trying to muffle the sound. His eyes slid closed as Radulfr started stroking him. The soft brush of Radulfr's thumb across the head of his cock made Ein shudder.

Ein curled his hands against Radulfr's thighs. He needed something to hold on to, something to keep him from screaming in delight. Every movement of Radulfr's hand on his aching shaft took him higher.

As his body overloaded on pure sensation, Ein turned his head and buried it in Radulfr's chest, sinking his teeth in. He heard Radulfr grunt but couldn't loosen his teeth. He felt like his entire body was seizing.

Then the most amazing feeling swept over Ein's body. He shuddered as his release shot out of his cock. Radulfr's hand tightened around him and continued to stroke him through his long orgasm. Ein slumped back against Radulfr, all the energy drained from his body. He felt languid, dreamy. He felt wonderful.

He could hear Radulfr panting behind him. The man's chest was rising and falling rapidly. Radulfr grabbed him by his hips and yanked him back until something long and hard pressed against Ein's back.

Ein tilted his head back and grinned up at Radulfr. He saw the man's eyebrows shoot up as he reached behind him and pressed his hands over Radulfr's cock. Ein watched Radulfr's eyes as he started moving his hand up and down Radulfr's hard length. The little flare in Radulfr's nostrils was the most amazing thing Ein had ever seen. He wanted to see more.

He tugged at the strings on Radulfr's pants, trying to get them undone. Suddenly, his hands were pushed out of the way. Ein bit his lip to keep from smiling as he looked straight ahead. He could feel Radulfr fumbling with the draws on his pants.

His hands were grabbed then pressed against hot, rigid flesh. Ein felt Radulfr stiffen when he wrapped his fingers around his thick erection. Radulfr started panting faster. Ein tilted his head, knowing what Radulfr needed. A moment later, Radulfr's face was buried in the nap of his neck.

"Gods, *kisa*, your hands feel so good," Radulfr whispered into his ear.

Ein grinned. He started rubbing one hand up and down Radulfr's cock. He reached down and cupped Radulfr's ball sac with the other.

He tried to be gentle, but every time he squeezed a little too hard, Radulfr's entire body shuddered.

Ein began to think Radulfr preferred bit of pain and started tugging on the man's ball sac a little harder. Radulfr went wild—well, as wild as a man trying to hide the fact he was fooling around under a cape could be.

Ein jerked when he felt Radulfr's teeth scrape along his neck. Radulfr's hands tightened around his waist. The man's legs stiffened. A deep growl sounded against Ein's throat and hot cream filled his hand, Radulfr shuddering several times.

"I wish I was balls deep in your ass right now," Radulfr murmured as he hugged Ein. "I'd fuck you into unconsciousness. You wouldn't sit comfortably for a week, Ein, I promise you."

Ein tilted his head back to look up Radulfr. "I'm not seeing the downside here."

He grinned when Radulfr roared with laughter. He didn't even mind the inquisitive looks he received from the others when he turned back around. That didn't mean his face didn't flush. Despite what Radulfr said, Ein suspected everyone knew exactly what they had been doing. He just couldn't bring himself to care.

* * * *

Ein groaned, sleep slipping away from him slowly. It took him a moment to figure out what woke him, and when he did, he inhaled swiftly and pushed back against the hard cock sinking into his ass inch by wonderful inch.

One of Radulfr's arms was wrapped around him. The other one held his leg up to his chest. Radulfr was using both as leverage as he thrust into Ein.

"Radulfr."

"Needed..." Radulfr panted softly, "couldn't wait."

"O–okay." Ein was all for not waiting.

"Love being inside you."

And Ein loved being filled by Radulfr. The man wasn't massive, but he was close. He filled every inch of Ein's ass. Ein felt like he was so full, he could feel Radulfr's heartbeat. The man surrounded him inside and out.

"Grab your leg, *kisa*."

Ein had no idea why Radulfr wanted him to hold his leg but did it anyway. His obedience was rewarded a moment later when Radulfr's free hand wrapped around his cock. Radulfr moved, leaning up to hunch over Ein a little. Ein felt the merits in that position immediately. It gave Radulfr better leverage to thrust into him.

Ein had only done this once before, the night Radulfr claimed him. He remembered it being intense, astounding. But this, knowing Radulfr wasn't fucking him because he had to, rather because he wanted to, made it even more passionate.

Ein could feel Radulfr's thrusts becoming more erratic, more powerful. He knew the man was getting close. He felt his own body moving closer to an orgasm also. His balls were drawing up tight against his body. His cock throbbed, leaking drops of pre-cum.

"Bite me, Radulfr," Ein whispered as he tilted his head to one side.

He knew Radulfr wanted it. He could feel the excitement in him, in the way Radulfr started pounding into him harder. Ein inhaled sharply at the pain that exploded in his neck as Radulfr's teeth sank into his throat.

The pain was fleeting, quickly swept away by pleasure so intense that Ein's vision blurred. Radulfr grunted and filled Ein with his release. The hot spurts shooting inside of him were enough to throw Ein over the edge.

He cried out, not caring who heard him, and came all over Radulfr's hand. Radulfr shuddered against Ein's back and slowly withdrew his teeth, licking at the bite mark. Ein sighed happily when he was pulled back against Radulfr's chest. He lowered his legs and just lay there, enjoying the afterglow as Radulfr caressed his skin, soothing him.

"You are indeed a gift from the gods, Ein."

"No." Ein glanced over his shoulder at Radulfr. "I'm just me."

"Don't play yourself for a fool, Ein." Radulfr smiled as he pushed the hair back from Ein's face. "You are a gift, never doubt that. I never dreamed I would find someone that eases my heart so much. I was truly blessed the day I accepted you in a peace-pledge."

Ein blinked rapidly as tears began to spring up in his eyes. He quickly looked away, not wanting Radulfr see him. It wasn't manly to cry, but he was just so affected by Radulfr's words. He never hoped to be wanted so much. He had been ready to settle for simply being accepted.

"You are precious to me, Ein," Radulfr whispered into Ein's ear. "Never doubt what you mean to me."

Ein swallowed hard. The lump building in his throat was making it hard to breath. "How can you know that?"

"I've learned to trust my instincts, Ein. They have kept me alive." Ein leaned into the hand Radulfr stroked down the side of his cheek. His hand felt so warm, so gentle. "My instincts tell me that you hold my heart."

"Me?"

"Yes, Ein, you." Radulfr chuckled. "You soothe me, *kisa*. You make me smile and laugh. You bring me unimaginable pleasure with your body or even the simple touch of your hand upon mine. You make my heart glad when you are near. And you make it drop to my toes when you are not."

The lump in Ein's throat grew bigger. He couldn't believe a man of Radulfr's stature was saying the things he was. Radulfr was a warrior, a jarl. He didn't lay his feelings out there for anyone, so why him?

"I… I was always afraid no one would want me," Ein admitted in a low whisper. "My *móðir* died on the day of my birth, killed by Jarl

Dagr for her indiscretion with my *faðir*. And my *faðir* cannot acknowledge me. Beyond *Godi* Asmundr, there has been no one that even cared if I lived or died."

"I do."

Radulfr grabbed Ein's chin and forced his face up. Ein's eyes widened at the strength he could see in Radulfr's eyes combined with a vulnerability that Ein would not have expected in the larger man.

"I care very much, Ein. I would be very upset if something were to happen to you." Radulfr's other arm tightened forcibly around Ein. "You accepted the *handsal* and became mine. I will not give you up without a fight."

"I'm not going anywhere, Radulfr," Ein hastened to assure Radulfr. "I belong to you now."

"And I'm keeping you."

Ein grunted when he was suddenly crushed in Radulfr's arms. He liked the fact that Radulfr felt so strong about him but… "Radulfr, can't breathe."

Radulfr chuckled as he loosened his arms. "Sorry, *kisa*."

"Radulfr." Vidarr was all of a sudden squatting down in front of them. "It's time to go. Riders have been spotted down in the ravine at the bottom of the hill."

Ein jerked in fear then suddenly remembered that he still had Radulfr's cock buried in his ass. His face flushed furiously as he groaned and pressed it in Radulfr's arm. Radulfr chuckled and slowly pulled back.

"We'll be right with you, Vidarr."

Vidarr grinned and pointed over his shoulder. "We'll just be over here getting the horses ready. Just try and hurry."

Ein waited until Vidarr walked away before turning over to glare at Radulfr. "He knew exactly what we were doing."

"He did. He just wishes he was doing the same thing."

Ein groaned. "Once, just once, I would like to do this without an audience."

"Come on, *kisa*," Radulfr said as he tossed the furs back and rolled to his feet then held out his hand. "If we're quick enough, we can get a couple of minutes at the brook to clean up."

Ein groaned and grabbed Radulfr's hand. He was surprised at how fast he was pulled to his feet. He quickly released Radulfr's hand and pulled his pants back up. He felt ridiculous when Radulfr laughed and tied his own pants closed.

He followed Radulfr across their makeshift camp to the small brook on the far side. A quick glance over his shoulder showed the rest of the warriors loading the horses and cleaning up the camp.

It made Ein feel better that everyone was kind of ignoring him and Radulfr as they cleaned up. He knew the men knew exactly what he and Radulfr had been up to. They were just being polite and pretending they hadn't seen a thing.

"Ready, *kisa*?"

Ein nodded and walked to the horse he had been riding before. He didn't get so scared this time when Radulfr lifted him up onto the horse's back, even if it was still a long ways off the ground. He just grabbed the horse's mane and held on until Radulfr climbed on behind him. Then he grabbed on to Radulfr.

"I need to teach you how to ride on your own, little one."

"No. I like riding with you."

"I like riding with you, too, but there may be a time when you need to ride without me. I want you to be prepared for anything."

"But—"

Ein rolled his eyes when Radulfr pressed his finger against his mouth. He really wished Radulfr would stop doing that. It was very aggravating.

"It's not an option, Ein. Your duty to me is to keep yourself safe. I need you to remind me what I fight for, what is wonderful in this world. I won't have that if something happens to you."

Ein heaved a large sigh. "Fine, I learn how to ride a horse. But does it have to be this horse? He's huge."

Radulfr chuckled and snapped the reins. "We can start you out on a smaller horse, but be forewarned, one day you will be able to ride this horse by yourself. If we're ever able to retrieve my horse, you need to be prepared. He's even bigger."

"Bigger?" Ein swallowed hard. He didn't see that as a good thing.

"You'll be fine, *kisa*. I would never do anything to bring you harm."

"I just…" Ein shook his head. "Swords and daggers and huge horses… it's all a little off-putting, Radulfr."

Radulfr patted Ein's arm. "It will be fine, little one, you'll see. We should reach my clan in a few days, and we'll be safe."

A cold shiver suddenly ran down Ein's spine like the hand of death tapping at him. He shivered and glanced around as the wind suddenly picked up and swept through the trees, blowing at them until they nearly bent in half. It was eerie.

Ein felt like it might be a sign of things to come. Something deep inside of him was telling Ein that things wouldn't be quite so easy for them when they reached Radulfr's clan, not like Radulfr planned.

"I hope you're right, Radulfr."

Chapter 10

Radulfr breathed his first big sigh of relief in days when he saw the top of the rise leading into the valley where his clan lived. They were finally home and safe. They had been lucky enough to stay ahead of whoever was hunting them, but just barely. It took a lot of hard riding and very little rest.

Everyone was dirty, hungry, and exhausted—especially Ein. He had stood up well under the stress, never complaining no matter how much Radulfr put him through. He just kept trudging ahead, accepting everything that came.

Radulfr was so proud of him he could burst. Ein was the perfect mate for him. He was sweet and kind, drawing out Radulfr's softer side. But Ein was also determined and fierce, willing to fight by his side as a mate should.

Radulfr couldn't wait to introduce Ein to his clan members. They might be a little put off by the fact that Ein was his bride and a man, but Radulfr knew they would accept him in time. Ein would be a great asset to the clan.

"Look." Radulfr pointed to the straw rooftops of the clan homes as they came over the rise. "That's home, Ein."

"We're here?" Ein sat up straighter.

"We are. This is our valley."

"It's bigger than I thought it would be."

"It's a big clan. We have almost three hundred men, women, and children. Many live in the middle of the village, but there are a few outlying farms." Radulfr pointed to a large building near the center of the village. "That's our *langhus* right over there."

"Do you live with others?"

"Vidarr and Haakon share the *langhus* with me right now. My *faðir* used to, but he recently moved in with a widow on the edge of town. There are a few freeman and thralls that come and go during the day, but I prefer to have privacy whenever I can."

Ein nodded, but Radulfr could feel his nervousness. He could see it. Ein kept looking left and right as if he expected someone to jump out at them any moment. Radulfr hugged Ein closer to his chest.

"We're safe, Ein."

Ein shook his head. "No, this is wrong. We shouldn't be here. We need to go."

Radulfr frowned. Ein sounded like he was ready to go into a full-blown panic. It was the first time since the whole insane situation started that Radulfr actually saw Ein become upset to this degree. Usually he just accepted things and moved on. Now, he was practically shaking apart in Radulfr's arms.

"Ein?"

"Please, can we go?" Ein's face was white as snow when he glanced back over his shoulder. "I don't want to be here."

Radulfr motioned with his hand for everyone to stop then brought his own horse to a standstill. Ein was so distressed that he couldn't ignore it. He handed the reins to Ein then slid from the horse.

"Stay quiet and stay still," he whispered to Ein.

Once Ein nodded, Radulfr motioned for Vidarr and Baldr to follow him as he moved to the bushes on the edge of the rise overlooking the small valley below. The closer to the edge he got, the farther down to the ground he went until he was crawling forward on his arms.

Radulfr didn't like what he saw when he reached the edge of the rise. The sun was in its highest position. There should have been people coming and going everywhere, but there wasn't a person in sight. There weren't even any dogs running around. There was nothing.

The more Radulfr looked, the more uneasy he became. He couldn't even see any smoke coming out of any houses. There was no noise. It was eerily silent. It was as if the entire village had just up and left, leaving everything exactly where it was.

Radulfr motioned with his hand then crawled back from the edge of the rise until he reached a point where he could stand up. Vidarr and Baldr joined him. Radulfr pushed his hand through his hair as he tried to decide what to do. Just riding into the village didn't seem like an option. Something was going on, and the longer Radulfr thought about it, the more concerned he grew.

"Ideas?" he asked as he looked at Vidarr and Baldr.

"We could just ride away but—" Baldr started.

Radulfr shook his head. "Not something I would be comfortable with. I need to know where my people are, if they are safe. I need someplace safe to take Ein."

"If you're intent on going in, then we need a plan," Baldr said. "Darkness isn't that far away. We can wait until then and sneak in, or you and your friends can ride on in like you don't know anything is wrong. They might not know about us."

"I won't bring any danger to Ein."

"No, no." Baldr shook his head. "That is not my plan. Ein can stay behind with Alimi while we go in."

"If they are expecting me to bring Ein home, then they are going to wonder why he isn't with us. However, Alimi isn't that much bigger than Ein, and no one here knows him. Alimi could pose as my mate."

Vidarr's hands fisted. "Alimi should stay here with Ein. Someone else can go in his place."

Radulfr rolled his eyes when Baldr snorted. "Baldr?"

"Alimi may seem a bit smaller than the rest of us, but don't underestimate the man. He's better at hand-to-hand combat than all of us here put together. The little fucker is quick on his feet and even quicker with a blade."

"An even better reason for him to stay behind with Ein," Vidarr said. "He can help protect Ein from harm."

Radulfr stared at Vidarr, confusion warring with his amazement. "Do you have something against Alimi?"

"No, of course not. I just—"

"I can handle myself."

Radulfr swung around to see Alimi standing behind him. A deep scowl covered his face and his arms crossed over his chest. Alimi looked pissed. And he was sending all of that anger directly at Vidarr.

"Alimi," Vidarr said, "I just wanted—"

"I know exactly what you wanted, and you can forget about it. I'm better equipped to go into a fight than you are, and it's about damn time you understood that."

"Alimi, please." Vidarr reached a hand out to the man. "Would just listen to me? It's not that I don't want you in a fight. I just think—"

"Actually, you're not thinking at all," Alimi said. "If you were, you would understand that I am a much better choice than anyone here. I am smaller than the others, and I have blond hair just like Ein. The only thing I'm missing is the pointed ears, and those are easily hidden."

"Damn it, Alimi!"

Radulfr's mouth dropped open when Vidarr reached over and grabbed Alimi by the arms and jerked him closer. Radulfr's eyebrows shot up when Vidarr kissed Alimi as if he was never going to let him breathe again. When Vidarr finally let him go, both men were panting.

"If you get hurt," Vidarr growled, "I will tan your hide."

"And if he doesn't," Haakon said as he walked up, "I will."

Radulfr felt like rubbing his eyes to see if he were truly seeing what he thought he was. Vidarr let Alimi go, only to release him to Haakon, who grabbed Alimi, swung him around, and kissed him just like Vidarr had. By the time Haakon let Alimi go a few moments later, the man was weaving a bit as if drunk. He just kind of stared up at Vidarr and Haakon in a daze.

Radulfr glanced over at Baldr when he heard a small chuckle. Baldr's lips were curled up in an amused smile. He gestured to the three men. "Did you know about this?"

"I suspected."

"And you didn't tell me because…?"

"I knew they would tell you when the time was right. Before now, Vidarr and Haakon were not ready to lay claim to Alimi. I believe they are now."

"Yes, I would say they just did."

Baldr chuckled. "Now it is just up to Alimi to decide if he wants to be claimed by them."

Radulfr glanced over to see his friends surrounding Alimi, pressing his slightly smaller body between theirs. He started to grin. "I'm not sure they are going to give him a choice. Vidarr and Haakon seemed to have made the decision for him."

"We'll see. Alimi is really not one to be taken lightly despite his smaller stature. I've spent a lot of winters in his company. He is stronger than he looks."

Radulfr had to wonder at that statement. Before he could ask, Ein walked over. He looked confused as he walked past at Vidarr, Haakon, and Alimi. When he reached Radulfr, he gestured back to the three men with his thumb.

"What is going on with them?"

Radulfr shrugged. "Long story, *kisa*. We'll talk about it later. In the meantime, I want you to stay here with Coinin. We need to ride down into the village and find out what's happened to our people."

Ein's face paled. "What? No, we can—"

"Ein," Radulfr said as he grabbed the smaller man by his shoulders, "this has to happen. I cannot leave my people unprotected. I have a duty to them. I need to go in there and find out what happened to them."

Ein sucked in his lower lip and bit down on it with his teeth. Radulfr could see the battle going on in Ein's expressive eyes. He gathered Ein into his arms and kissed the top of his head.

"Now, you listen to me, little one," he said quietly. "I have too much to live for to let anything happen to me. I won't do anything that will separate us. I am also very good at what I do. I need you to stay here and stay safe so I can concentrate on what needs to be done without worrying about you."

Radulfr leaned back and reached for Ein's chin, tilting the man's face back. "Can you do that for me?"

Ein pressed his lips together for a moment as if he was going to argue but then he nodded. "Just come back to me, preferably in one piece."

"On my honor, *kisa*."

Since he had Ein's face tilted up anyway, Radulfr leaned in and took a kiss—a long, thoughtful, heartfelt kiss. His lips pressed against Ein's then gently covered his mouth, exploring and savoring the sweet taste of his mate.

Radulfr enjoyed the dazed look in Ein's eyes when he lifted his head. He rubbed his thumb over Ein's swollen lips. "I'll be back soon, *kisa*."

It took every ounce of Radulfr's willpower to turn away from Ein and walk to his horse. He grabbed the horse's mane and pulled himself up. Radulfr's fingers clenched in the long strands of hair when he looked at Ein one more time.

Ein stood there, still looking dazed. He was absently rubbing his fingers over his just-kissed lips as if trying to relive the kiss. When his eyes lifted and landed on Radulfr, Ein blinked several times. He didn't say a word, just raised his hand in farewell.

Radulfr waved back then made himself turn away. He glanced over at Coinin. "Keep him safe, Coinin."

Coinin nodded. Radulfr wasn't surprised. He had barely heard more than a word out of the man since they met. Coinin was not a talker. Radulfr nodded back and waited for the others to get on their horses.

He refused to look back at Ein as he started down the hill into his valley. He just couldn't. If he did, he wasn't sure he would be able to ride away. Leaving Ein felt wrong, but he knew he needed to keep the man safe. Until he knew what was happening with his people, Ein wouldn't be safe there.

Radulfr took the lead, Alimi right behind him, Vidarr and Haakon bringing up the rear. He hoped nothing was wrong, but he knew it was an empty hope. Something was definitely wrong. The feeling of unease grew the closer he rode to the village.

Radulfr slowed his horse when he reached the first building in the village, a small *langhus* belonging to a goat herder and his wife. There were goats in the pen beside the house. That in itself worried Radulfr. They should have been out grazing, not in their pens.

Radulfr turned around to see if Vidarr and Haakon had seen what he did. They both nodded and continued to watch as they followed behind him. Radulfr waved Alimi forward. When the man rode up next to him, he nodded toward the pen then shook his head. Alimi glanced at the goat pen and nodded.

Radulfr continued on toward the center of the village, winding through the dirt streets. He paused when he reached the end of the road. It opened up into a large open area, the center of the village. Radulfr's *langhus* sat directly across from him.

It was eerily silent.

Radulfr climbed off his horse. He grabbed the reins from Alimi and started leading the two horses toward his *langhus*. Radulfr's steps faltered when the door to his *langhus* creaked open and his *faðir*, Halldor, stepped out.

"*Faðir*, I hope all is well?"

"Radulfr." His *faðir* nodded at him and clasped his hands together in front of him. "You've brought your betrothed home with you, I see."

Radulfr watched his *faðir* carefully. It wasn't usual for the man to greet him when he came home. Radulfr didn't exactly get along with his *faðir*. They hadn't been close since Radulfr's *móðir* died. Radulfr didn't blame his *faðir*, but he didn't make excuses for the man's harsh treatment when growing up, either.

"I have, although Jarl Dagr was not as truthful as I had hoped."

"There is issue with your betrothed?"

"I'd rather discuss that inside. I do not believe it is fit for everyone's ears."

Radulfr wasn't surprised when his *faðir* gave a slight shake of his head. He knew someone was waiting inside. He cocked an eyebrow. His *faðir* nodded then held down four fingers. Radulfr nodded back, just a slight dip of his head, though. He didn't know if they were being watched or not.

"Is everyone out in the fields, *Faðir*?" Radulfr asked. "This conversation doesn't need to be overheard by others until we decide what to do with my betrothed."

"Surely you're not thinking of negating the *handsal*?"

"No, I gave my word of honor, but that doesn't mean I'm not going to take this out of Jarl Dagr's hide. He knew Ein was a man when he brought up the peace-pledge. I may just have to pay him a visit."

Halldor eyes widened, and he gave a slight shake of his head again. He looked almost terrified. Radulfr guessed that Jarl Dagr was somehow involved in whatever was going on. The man was probably waiting for him inside.

"Let's take this inside, *Faðir*." Radulfr walked back to Alimi's horse and helped the man down. He hoped Alimi would follow his lead and play dumb. "I'd rather have a chance to make a plan before we introduce Ein to the clan."

One of the things Radulfr always liked about living in a *langhus* was the fact that it was usually just one large room. The instant he stepped inside, he knew they were in trouble. Three armed men stood there with their swords at the throats of a few villagers. A fourth man sat by the fire drinking something from a cup. Radulfr instantly recognized the man and nearly growled.

"Fafnir, what brings you to my village?"

"I've come to collect your betrothed, Radulfr." Fafnir stood up and shook the last few drops of liquid out of his cup.

"My betrothed?"

"It seems my *faðir* failed to mention Ein in all the years he's been alive. I never even knew about him."

"And what does that have to do with my betrothed?"

Fafnir waved his hand. "Why don't you bring your friends inside where they can be warm? I imagine it's mighty cold outside right now. Besides, I'm interested in meeting this man you have peace-pledged with."

Radulfr stepped inside a few more steps. He heard Alimi, Vidarr, and Haakon step inside after him. Fafnir waved his hand again and one of the other soldiers walked over. He quickly gathered everyone's weapons and carried them back to Fafnir.

"Please, join me in a drink."

Radulfr grit his teeth and walked over to stand next to Fafnir. "I ask you again, Fafnir, what does any of this have to do with my betrothed?"

"So impatient."

Radulfr clenched his fists to keep from reaching for the man. He was angry enough to rip Fafnir limb from limb with his bare hands. He just hoped his anger didn't get away from him. He didn't want to shift into what he had been before, at least not until he knew what Fafnir was playing at.

"You wanted to talk about my betrothed." Radulfr crossed his arms over his chest. "So, talk."

"I want him."

"Not happening," Radulfr said. "I gave my word of honor to accept the peace-pledge."

"Your word of honor." Fafnir rolled his eyes and pointed to one of the villagers sitting on their knees across the room. "Is your honor going to save them from death?"

Radulfr stiffened when one of Fafnir's soldiers placed his sword across the throat of the villager. "Fafnir, be warned now, if even one of my clan dies at your hand or the hand of one of your soldiers, I will watch you die slowly."

"You seem to believe that you have a choice here, jarl. You don't." Fafnir turned to look at Alimi. Something purely evil crossed his face. "I will have Ein."

"Is this because of the *heiman fylgia*?"

"No." Fafnir laughed. "My *faðir* has already provided me with the funds to pay the bride price."

"That's not what we agreed upon. The *heiman fylgia* is your responsibility."

Fafnir waved his hand in dismissal. "Paying the bride price is the least of my worries. Ein is worth much more than any amount of silver due to you. He's the *sonr* of a god."

Chapter 11

Ein paced back and forth a few feet away from the horses and Coinin. He wrung his hands together as he glanced over the edge of the rise into the valley below. He was worried about Radulfr, more worried than he was when they were being attacked by the creek side. Then, he could see what was going on.

Currently, he could only guess. And his imagination was running wild. Images of Radulfr being in a sword fight filled his head, making him even more anxious.

"Ein."

Ein swung around expecting to see Coinin looking in his direction, but the man was still standing there, looking out over the rise just as he had been doing. "Coinin, did you say something?"

Ein frowned when Coinin turned and shook his head then went back to watching the valley below. Maybe he was hearing things.

"Ein."

Fear started to build a lump on Ein's throat as he swung around again. He knew he wasn't hearing things this time. Someone was calling out to him. He searched the small rise and spotted a flash of brown fabric near the edge of some trees.

Curious but cautious, Ein walked toward the trees. His heart nearly leapt out of his chest when a man in brown robes stepped out from behind one of the trees. Ein pressed his hand against his chest and panted rapidly.

"Hello, Ein."

"Hello, *Faðir*."

"How have you been?"

Ein gaped. "That's all you have to say? I haven't seen you in ages. Every time you want me to know something, you send *grandfaðir*. You never come yourself."

"I know, and I'm sorry, *sonr*." Freyr, the god of fertility, love, and phallic objects, grimaced. "I did not want it to be this way, but my good wife cannot look past my indiscretion with your *móðir*. She makes things…unpleasant when I come to visit you."

Ein sighed. He knew things were never going to be different with his *faðir*. They were what they were, and he had long ago given up being accepted by his *faðir's* family. Besides, he had a new family in Radulfr now.

"So, why have you come?"

Freyr crossed his arms behind his back and began pacing. Ein's eyebrows shot up in surprise. He'd never seen his *faðir* pace before. The man was actually frowning as if something was bothering him.

"*Faðir*, what's wrong?"

"We have a problem that needs to be dealt with, Ein—a grave problem."

"What?" Ein started getting nervous.

Freyr looked over at Ein. His face was serious, not a hint of amusement anywhere. "You mixed up the vials, Ein."

"What vials?"

"The gold and silver vials that your *grandfaðir* gave you."

Ein suddenly remembered the two vials, one gold, one silver. He remembered his *grandfaðir* giving him strict instructions on their use, but he couldn't remember what exactly those instructions were.

"Okay, so what's the problem then?"

"Those vials were meant to give you long life and good health, Ein. The silver vial contained the elixir of life. The gold vial contained the white drops of immortality. Combined, they are meant to make you immortal."

Ein blinked. "You made me immortal?"

"That was the intention, Ein, but you didn't use them as instructed."

Ein's eyebrows drew together as he tried to decipher his *faðir's* cryptic words. His *faðir* never spoke directly, but in riddles. It was aggravating as hell. "So, what…am I going to die now?"

"Damn it, Ein, you're not listening to me." Freyr's face turned red with rage. "You mixed up the vials. They were supposed to give you long life. Instead, they have made it so you can create life."

"What?" Ein whispered.

"You and your *Berserkr* have created a child."

Ein stared for a moment as the shock of his *faðir's* words rolled through then he began to shake his head, slowly backing away. Ein knew the gods often played tricks on mortals, especially Loki, but he never expected it from his *faðir*.

"No, you've lost your senses," Ein said. "Men don't carry children."

"They do now!" Freyr exclaimed as he tossed his hands up into the air. "You've done the one thing that no god has ever been able to do, Ein. You've created life between two men."

Ein dropped to the ground when his shaking legs gave out. He suddenly felt very cold and wrapped his arms around himself. He wanted Radulfr. He wanted to know he wasn't losing his mind. It just wasn't possible what his *faðir* was saying.

"You have to be wrong," Ein whispered when his *faðir* knelt down in front of him. He raised his eyes to meet his *faðir's*. "You've been spending time with Loki, right? You're playing with me."

"No, *sonr*, I'm not," Freyr said softly. The smile that spread across his lips was rueful, saddened. "I would never trick you in this manner. I do not believe even Loki would do such a thing."

"Bu–but how?"

"The gold and silver vials, Ein."

Ein frowned. He felt dazed, light-headed. He pushed his hair back from his face. "What now? I mean, how am I supposed to give birth? I'm not equipped to carry a child."

"I know, *sonr*." Freyr frowned. "I believe the best thing for everyone is if this doesn't happen."

"What? No!" Ein shouted. Horror didn't even begin to describe the feeling racing through him at a breakneck speed. He wrapped one arm around his stomach to protect the child and scrambled away from his *faðir*. "You're not going to take this child from me!"

"Ein, be reasonable," Freyr said as he stood to his feet and started toward Ein. "It's for the best. Men are not meant to have children like this."

"No!"

Yes, Ein was shocked by what had transpired, but he wasn't about to take the easy road and kill Radulfr's child, no matter how strange it was to be carrying one. This was still Radulfr's child.

"Ein, this is not up for debate," Freyr said. "I cannot allow you to have this child. The gods would be furious."

"I don't care," Ein shouted as he climbed to his feet. "You're not taking it from me."

Freyr raised his hand and the wind began to blow roughly through the trees. Leaves began to blow through the air. Ein's hair whipped wildly around his face. He knew his *faðir* was attempting to scare him by using his god powers. Ein refused to be intimidated.

"No!" he shouted, but his words were lost in the harsh wind.

Ein turned to run, but a large gust of wind caught him and pulled him back to his *faðir*. Somehow, Ein just knew if his *faðir* touched him, it would be all over. Freyr would take the child from him—just a single touch.

"Ein, *sonr*, don't make this more difficult than it has to be."

Ein struggled against the wind pulling him backwards toward his *faðir*. He felt tears start to stream down his face as he fought to get away. Desperate sobbing noises fell from his lips.

"Please, no," he cried out as he was dragged to his knees.

Ein cringed away from his *faðir* as the man walked up and squatted down in front of him. Freyr reached out to touch his face, but Ein jerked back. He didn't want his *faðir* to touch him. His *faðir* hadn't seemed to care when he was growing up. Why should he care now?

"I am sorry, Ein," Freyr said. "I wish it could be another way."

"Don't do this, please."

Ein knew he was begging. He didn't care. He couldn't let his *faðir* take something so precious away from him and Radulfr. Ein had no idea how Radulfr would react, but he couldn't give up proof of the feelings between the two of them, not without a fight.

"I have to, Ein."

"No!" Ein screamed as Freyr reached for him. He raised his hands to ward his *faðir* off.

Ein's jaw dropped open in shock as his *faðir* was suddenly tossed across the small grassy area as if he weighed no more than a feather. Ein watched Freyr crash to the ground then lay there unmoving.

He stared for a moment, waiting for Freyr to move or something. He climbed to his feet, unsure, hesitant, and then slowly started walking toward his *faðir*. As scared as he was of what the man might do, Freyr was still his *faðir*.

"Faðir?" he whispered as he knelt down next to the man. When he didn't receive a response, Ein reached over and shook his *faðir's* shoulder. *"Faðir?"*

Ein jumped back and looked around wildly when his *faðir* suddenly disappeared from sight. He started breathing rapidly, pressing his hand against his chest. He wanted Radulfr.

"Ein."

Ein flipped around so fast that he fell down on his butt in the dirt. *"Grandfaðir?"*

Njörðr smiled and reached out a hand to Ein. Ein just stared at it, afraid to take it, afraid that his *grandfaðir* wanted the same thing that his *faðir* did. Njörðr squatted down and clasped his hands together between his knees.

"Ein, despite his status as a god, your *faðir* does not always know what is best." Njörðr held out his hand. "I promise upon my honor as god of *Vanaheimr* that I will in no way, through deed or thought, harm your unborn child."

When Njörðr held his hand out a second time, Ein took it. He was pulled to his feet then dusted off. Ein looked around but could see no sign of his *faðir*. "Where did he go?"

"Your *faðir*?"

Ein nodded.

"I sent him home." Njörðr sighed deeply, clasping his hands together again, this time behind his back. Njörðr was a very serious god. "Your *faðir* has not the sight, Ein. He does not understand the importance of this child to the gods. He listens to his wife too much, tries to please her to make up for his many indiscretions."

"What do you mean?" Ein covered his abdomen again as if his simple touch could ward off whatever might happen to the unborn child he carried. "What importance?"

"Your *sonr*…" Njörðr gestured to Ein's stomach, "is the *sonr* of a *Berserkr* and a *demi-god*. He will have your heart and Radulfr's strength. Remember what I told you. You and Radulfr are meant for great things."

"Yes, but I thought…" Ein frowned. "I thought you meant Radulfr's transformation into a *Berserkr*."

"No, *grandsonr*, that is only part of the equation. This child will end the struggle between the *Æsir* and the *Vanir*. The *Æsir–Vanir War* ended many winters ago, but the struggle still continues."

"How can my *sonr* do anything?" Ein asked. "He's not even born yet."

Njörðr smiled and placed his hand upon Ein's abdomen. "He will join us soon. Óðinn and I have both foreseen it. Your *sonr* will be descended from a *Berserkr*, who is of Óðinn's creation. You, my *grandsonr*, are a *demi-god*, part *álfar*. Your *sonr* will be both *Æsir* and the *Vanir*. He will unite the gods themselves."

Ein blinked. He opened his mouth to say something then realized he had no idea what to say. What could he say? His *grandfaðir* just told him that his *sonr*, created with another man, would be the savior of the gods.

"Now come, Ein. It is time to go rescue your Radulfr. He is in great danger. A band of Jarl Dagr's men are riding in from the North. They have joined up with those that have hunted you these last few days. You have until dawn to gather what you can and leave this area. You are not to return."

"This is Radulfr's home. His people are here. We can't leave."

"You must, Ein. Your child is not safe here."

Tears started to rise up in Ein's eyes. Radulfr was going to hate him. "Where are we to go?"

"Ride south for three full moons then east for two more. Along the Volga River, you will find a large stronghold carved into the side of a mountain. *Novgarð* is large enough to hold any that decide to come with you and Radulfr."

"*Novgarð?*"

"Yes, Ein, and this is very important," Njörðr said. "You must listen to me very carefully. As long as you remain inside the walls of this stronghold, no harm can come to you, your child, or any that dwell inside. Óðinn and I have made *Novgarðr* a *frið-garðr*, an area of peace. You will be safe there."

Ein nodded. He understood what Njörðr was saying. He just didn't know if he was going to end up on some stronghold built by the gods. He wouldn't go anywhere without Radulfr. And if Radulfr didn't want to leave, he wouldn't.

"Ein, not even your *faðir* can get to you inside of *Novgarð*."

Ein paused for a moment and glanced up at his *grandfaðir*. "Why does he hate my child so much?"

Njörðr grimaced then patted Ein's shoulder. "He does not hate your child, Ein. Never think that. Freyr has spent many years trying to win back the favor of his wife. She has persuaded him that their lives can never come together again if your child is born."

"Why?" Ein cried out.

"Because you and your child are proof of Freyr's infidelity, your child even more so as it will be Freyr's first *grandsonr*. Gerðr cannot stand that. While she has been able to make mischief in your life while you lived at the *hov*, it was a sacred place, and she could not kill you. But now, you have left that sacred place. You are no longer protected."

Ein rubbed the tears from his eyes. He felt so alone in that moment. "Maybe it would have been better if Freyr just let Jarl Dagr kill me at birth. Then we could have avoided all of this."

"No so, *grandsonr*, not so." Njörðr wrapped an arm around Ein's shoulders and gave him a slight squeeze. "We would have missed so many wonderful conversations if you had died. And I so enjoy our conversations. Despite how guilty your *faðir* feels for his indiscretions, you are still my *grandsonr* and always will be. Never forget that. You are descended from the gods, Ein."

"How is that supposed to mean anything when so many people are trying to destroy me, including gods?"

"Just reach *Novgarð* and you will be safe."

"*If*, don't you mean, *if* I reach it?"

"Óðinn and I will not let you fail." Njörðr smiled, leaned in, and kissed Ein on the forehead then pushed him toward Coinin and the horses. "Now, go, my *grandsonr*. Rescue your mate and get yourself to the stronghold. Óðinn and I will come when the baby is due to be born and help you deliver him."

Ein didn't even want to think about delivering a baby. That was too far out of his realm of what he could currently deal with. Right now, he just wanted to go find Radulfr and feel the man's arms wrap around him. A week in bed with his mate didn't sound so bad either.

"Coinin," Ein said as he walked up to the man.

Coinin turned, smiling at Ein. He didn't seem freaked out by anything or even nervous. Ein got the impression that Coinin hadn't seen either Freyr and Njörðr's visits. Gods had a strange way about them.

"We need to go," Ein said as he reached for the reins of the horse he had ridden with Radulfr. He was going to get a riding lesson whether he wanted one or not. "More soldiers are coming. We need to warn Radulfr and the others."

"More soldiers?" Coinin started looking around. "Where?"

"Just take my word for it. They are coming."

Ein would have told Coinin, but he didn't think the man would believe him. He was just hoping that Radulfr would. Ein grabbed a handful of the horse's mane and swung up onto his back. He was surprised at how easy it was until he felt a gust of wind blow past him.

He chuckled and started his horse down the road into the valley. The gods might be strange, but they could be helpful when they were not trying to kill him. It was just too bad that they were so ready to kill him.

Ein flicked the reins of his horse. He wanted to go faster. He caught a flash of something out of the corner of his eyes and turned. Coin had shifted and was running along side of him. Soon, two other wolves joined them as they rode into the village.

Ein slowed his horse. He wasn't sure which *langhus* was Radulfr's. He didn't want to go into the wrong one. Luckily, Baldr, Ulfr, and Coinin started sniffing at each door then running to the next *langhus* and the next.

When Baldr stopped at one and whined as he looked over his shoulder, Ein knew they had found the right one. He stopped his horse a few feet from the *langhus* and climbed off, tying the reins to a nearby bush.

Ein drew in a deep breath for courage then walked up to the door. He pushed it open without knocking. The three wolves followed in behind him. Ein made it inside about two steps before he was spotted.

Three soldiers raised their swords in the air and started toward him. Radulfr shouted his name. Alimi shifted into a wolf. The villagers on the far side of the *langhus* cringed back in horror. All hell broke loose.

Ein pulled his dagger out to defend himself if need be. He could see Radulfr fighting with another man. Their swords clanked together making a horrendous noise. The wolves had Ein surrounded, growling and snarling at anyone who stepped too close. Ein had to just stand there and watch, his heart pounding rapidly.

He gripped the dagger in his hand so tightly that he felt the engraved handle bite into his fingers. Radulfr looked like he was getting tired. His opponent's sword was coming closer and closer to Radulfr's head with each lunge.

Ein pressed his free hand against his throat and took a step closer to Radulfr. He couldn't just stand there and watch his lover get hurt and possibly die. He had to do something. He tried to step around the large wolves, but they pinned him in at every turn until Ein tipped his head back and screamed out his frustration.

When he stopped screaming, he noticed that all sound in the room had stopped. He lowered his head and looked around. Everyone had stopped fighting. They looked frozen in place as they stared at him.

Finally, Radulfr and the man he was fighting lowered their swords. The other soldiers stepped back, watching him carefully. Even the wolves turned to look at him. Radulfr took a step closer to him.

"You have something to say, Ein?"

"Stop," Ein whispered.

"I cannot, *kisa*." Radulfr waved his sword toward his opponent. "Fafnir wishes to take you from me. I cannot allow that."

Ein glanced over at the sandy-haired man. "You are Fafnir, *sonr* of Jarl Dagr?"

The man's lips twisted together for a moment. The look he gave Ein made his skin crawl. He felt like he was on display at the marketplace. Fafnir wasn't just looking at him, he was appraising him.

"I am."

"Your *faðir* killed my *móðir*."

Fafnir shrugged. "These things happen."

"It does not bother you that she was your *móðir* also?"

"I don't remember her," Fafnir said. "It happened many winters past."

Ein thought Fafnir was a cold man, without a conscience. He didn't even seem bothered by the fact that his *faðir* killed their *móðir*. It was as if the entire thing didn't affect him one little bit. It gave Ein the chills.

"You are an ugly, ugly man."

Fafnir arched an eyebrow. "It matters not what you think, half-breed. It only matters what you can bring me from the gods. I imagine with you at my side, the gods will give me anything that I want." Fafnir laughed harshly and waved his hand around the *langhus*. "I will no longer be forced to live the life of a peasant. I will live in a castle made of gold."

"You've lost your mind if you think I will give you anything."

"Oh, not you, Ein, your *faðir*." Fafnir laughed again. "Oh yes, my *faðir* told me all about you and your connection with the gods. Your *faðir* will pay greatly to keep your head on your shoulders."

"I will never do anything you want."

"We will see how you feel about that when my *faðir* arrives. Your precious Radulfr will be no more, and as much as my *faðir* hates you, I will be your only solace."

"My precious Radulfr will kill you before you can touch a hair on my head." Ein knew it without a doubt. He dismissed Fafnir and turned to look at Radulfr. "We need to talk."

"*Kisa*, I'm in the middle of a sword fight." Radulfr waved his sword in the air. "Can this wait?"

Chapter 12

Ein was pale. His hands were shaking, both the one that gripped the dagger and the one he had pressed against his collarbone. He looked ready to fall apart. Radulfr debated going to him until he saw Fafnir move out of the corner of his eye.

"Ein, I really need you to stay where you are until this is over," Radulfr said as he raised his sword and pointed it at Fafnir.

"I can't." Ein drew in a deep breath and held it. "My *faðir* and *grandfaðir* came to see me while I was waiting for you to return. We have a problem. Well, actually, we have a few problems."

"What sort of problems?" Radulfr asked without looking away from Fafnir.

"There's another band of Jarl Dagr's soldiers coming. They will be here by dawn."

Radulfr almost groaned. He could hear Fafnir laughing and saw the delight on his face. More soldiers meant more fighting. At this point, Radulfr didn't even know how many of his villagers were still alive, if any beyond those in the *langhus*.

"I understand, Ein, but I can't leave without my people."

"There's more, Radulfr."

"I'm sure there is, but I'm a little busy at the moment, Ein. Can you give me a moment to kill Fafnir and his soldiers? Then you will have my full attention."

Radulfr could have shouted with glee when Ein replied, "Please, just hurry and get it over with. Our time here is short."

Radulfr cast a quick glance out of the corner of his eye to ensure that Ein was safely out of the way then lunged with his sword. Fafnir looked surprised but raised his sword just in time to save his head from being sliced off.

Radulfr had to admit that Fafnir was a well-trained swordsman, but he was also too cocky in his abilities. He took too many chances. Radulfr was able to get in several lucky shots before Fafnir started a campaign of his own, one meant to throw Radulfr off his game.

"My *faðir* is coming, jarl. He will be here by dawn."

"You will be dead by then, Fafnir."

"Will I?" Fafnir asked. "Or will I be better acquainting myself with your betrothed? He's attractive enough for a half-breed. I imagine I can still teach him a thing or two about being *sorðinn.*"

Radulfr growled and swung without thought. It earned him a deep cut across his arm. He could see what Fafnir was trying to do. Unfortunately, it was working. No one insulted his mate or threatened him without paying the price.

"You will never touch a hair on Ein's head."

"His hair holds not my interest." Fafnir laughed harshly. "His ass, however, is a different story."

Radulfr growled and lunged again, receiving a cut across his other arm.

"Is it a nice ass, jarl?" Fafnir asked as he raised his sword. "Does he take your cock sweetly or does he fight you? I prefer when they fight. It arouses me and makes my cock hard. Will your little mate fight me when I fuck him?"

Radulfr saw red. Fafnir had just gotten the fight he was looking for. Radulfr roared and dropped his sword to the ground. He heard shouts and screams as he let the shift come over him and transformed into the monster Fafnir had created with his words.

Radulfr felt his jaw elongate and his canines drop down. Dark fur sprouted up along his skin until he was covered from head to toe. Sharp claws grew out of the end of his fingers. He stood on two feet but had the look of half man, half wolf. He was *Berserkr*.

Fafnir's eyes widened and he swung out with his sword. Radulfr felt it hit him in the arm but felt no pain. He was surprised when he looked down and found no wound. Fafnir's sword had not penetrated his skin.

Radulfr swiped his clawed hand across Fafnir's torso. He howled when bright red began to blossom across Fafnir's shirt, a sure indication that the man was wounded. He struck again and again until Fafnir's sword fell to the ground and the man backed away, clutching at his chest.

"You have threatened my mate," Radulfr growled. "You have threatened everything I hold dear. You will die."

Fafnir screamed and took off running, his three soldiers running behind him. Ein dove out of the way as the wolves surrounding him took the four men down. He covered his face and looked away from the ensuing carnage.

"Ein, come."

Ein raised his head and ran, dodging the wolves and their prey. He ran right across the room and into Radulfr's arms, not seeming to care that Radulfr wasn't quite human at the moment.

Radulfr sighed deeply as he enfolded Ein in his arms and breathed in the man's sweet cleansing scent. All seemed to be right when he held Ein in his arms. Radulfr hugged Ein for several moments until he heard a loud howl.

He glanced up to see Baldr, Ulfr, Alimi, and Coinin all standing over what used to be Fafnir and his soldiers. They tossed their heads back and let out loud howls that sent chills of victory down Radulfr's spine.

"Baldr, remove the bodies, please," Radulfr said. "This mess is not fit for Ein's eyes."

Baldr barked and the wolves began dragging the dead bodies out the door. Radulfr returned his attention to the man in his arms. He leaned back and stroked his furred hand down the side of Ein's face, smiling when Ein leaned right into his hand.

"You are safe, *kisa*?"

"Define safe."

Radulfr chuckled. "You are unhurt?"

"For now, what the future holds, only the gods know."

Radulfr tapped the end of Ein's nose. "Yet another thing we must discuss."

Ein grimaced and nodded.

"Radulfr, what has become of you, my *sonr*?"

Radulfr looked up to see his *faðir* standing several feet away. "*Faðir*?"

"What is the meaning of this?" Radulfr's *faðir* waved his hand up and down, gesturing to his furry body. "What has happened to you?"

"I am a *Berserkr*. It is a gift from the gods."

The man shook his head, looking part afraid and part disgusted. "This is not a gift from the gods, Radulfr. This is a *geas*."

"Radulfr is not cursed," Ein shouted as he swung around to glare. "Radulfr has been gifted by the gods, in more ways than you can imagine. You have no right to treat him as if he is a *geas*."

"Shh, *kisa*." Radulfr gently patted Ein's shoulder. "My *faðir* has a right to his opinions. We knew when this happened that not everyone would be accepting of it."

"It's wrong, Radulfr." Ein's eyes were filled with angry tears when he turned to look at him. "The gods have chosen you for great things, for special things. Your *faðir* doesn't have the right to go against that."

"He's not, Ein. He just doesn't understand."

"And we don't have time to explain it to him." Ein tugged on Radulfr's shirt. "We have to leave, Radulfr. We only have until dawn."

Radulfr frowned. "Ein, my people are here. I can't just leave them unprotected."

More tears began to fill Ein's eyes. "We have to," he whispered.

"Not only is your mate a *sansorðinn*," Radulfr's *faðir* snapped, "he is *huglausi*, cowardly. You should have killed him instead of claiming him. Even the lawspeaker would have understood."

Radulfr pushed Ein behind him and grabbed for his *faðir's* throat at the same time. He lifted the man several inches off the ground and growled, baring his sharp canines.

"You do not threaten my mate."

"You mated a *sansorðinn*, a man that is willing to be sexually used by other men." Radulfr's *faðir* spit on the floor. "You have become a *meyla krafla mikli thur syr.*"

Radulfr roared at the insult to his *móðir* and tossed his *faðir* across the room. "I am not a child born of a long-dead sow. My *móðir* was a good woman who loved me until the day she died."

"She would be spinning in her grave right now if she could see you," the man said as he climbed to his feet and brushed his hand across his face. "You have brought shame to this clan."

Radulfr started to take a step toward his *faðir*, ready to rip the man apart, when he felt a hand on his arm. He looked down to see Ein holding him back.

"Please, Radulfr, don't. No matter what he says or what he has done, you would never forgive yourself. You're angry and upset right now. Calm your temper then deal with him." Ein began stroking his fingers over Radulfr's furry arm. "Besides, we have greater things to deal with than your *faðir.*"

Radulfr turned to growl at his *faðir* one last time then turned away from him. "He is no longer my *faðir*. Anyone that threatens my mate does not deserve to be acknowledged by me."

Ein swallowed hard and glanced away. "I understand your reasoning, but it still saddens me to come between you and your family."

Radulfr lifted Ein's chin with his hand "You are my family, Ein. You and Vidarr and Haakon and the others. If my *faðir* doesn't want to be part of our family, we will make our own." Radulfr thought Ein would be thrilled by his words. He frowned, concerned when Ein blanched instead. "Ein?"

"About that making our own family thing..." Ein swallowed again and glanced down at his hands, wringing them together. His little blond eyebrows drew together. "It seems I got the vials mixed up and—"

"Vials? What vials?"

"My *grandfaðir* gave me two vials the day he told me of your coming, one gold and one silver. They were meant to give me long life..." Ein shrugged. "Make me immortal or something, but I mixed them up and...and..."

"And what, kisa?"

There was a look of desperation in Ein's smoky gray-silver eyes when he looked up. He looked like he was about to lose his best friend.

"Ein?"

"I...I mixed up the vials and...and instead of making me mortal, it made me..." Ein licked his lips. "They were supposed to give me long life. Instead, they made it so I can create life, so we can create life."

Radulfr blinked. "What?"

Ein stared right into Radulf's eyes, his look so intent that Radulfr felt like Ein was looking into his soul. "I'm going to have a child," Ein whispered, "your child."

Radulfr tried not to move, to not utter a single sound as he took in Ein's words. They were the most outlandish words he had ever heard, even more than when Baldr tried to tell him he was a *Berserkr*. Baldr's words sounded more plausible.

Ein's eyes began to fill with tears when Radulfr didn't reply. He started to pull away. Radulfr could see the devastation his silence was bringing to the smaller man. As shocked as he was, he couldn't have that.

Radulfr yanked Ein close to his chest and hugged him, burying his face in Ein's sunlight-blond hair. He rocked Ein back and forth. "We'll figure this out, Ein, together."

"I'm sorry," Ein murmured.

"I'm not." Radulfr leaned back and tilted Ein's face up to his. "You've been a surprise to me from the very beginning but not one I have regretted. If this is what the gods wanted for us, then we will be happy about it and accept it as the gift it is."

"I didn't mean for this to happen."

Radulfr smiled. He was still in a state of shock but slowly warming to the idea that Ein could carry their child, especially since he never thought he could have children once he claimed Ein as his.

"Obviously, it was meant to happen, Ein."

Ein sniffed then smoothed his hand down the ragged edges of Radulfr's torn shirt. "You didn't sign on for this. I know that. I wouldn't blame you if—"

"You can stop that thought right there, Ein." Radulfr clenched his jaw. He grabbed Ein by his forearms and gave him a little shake. "I'm not going anywhere and neither are you. We accepted each other and that means we stay together no matter what."

"But, you—"

Radulfr frowned at Ein's words. "Do you want to leave me?"

"No!" Ein wrapped his fingers in the shredded fabric of Radulfr's shirt. His eyes widened, desperation making them darken. "I love you. I don't want to leave you."

Radulfr smiled, feeling at peace for the first time since they reached the valley. "I love you, too, *Kisa*."

"Some warrior you've turned out to be," snapped a voice from a few feet away. Halldor waved his hand in the air, his face twisted in disgust. "Look at you, the big strong jarl. You're worse than a woman."

Radulfr growled as he looked at his *faðir*. "What do you know about it, old man? You haven't fought a day in nearly twenty years.

You were more than happy to turn the clan over to me so you could drown your sorrows in a mug of mead. You haven't been sober more than a day since I was ten years old."

"At least I was a true warrior," Halldor sneered. "You…I don't even know what you are. You've taken to acting like a woman, professing your love for another man. You're disgusting. You're worse than a *fuðflogi*."

"I have not shunned marriage," Radulfr shouted. "I accepted my duty and took Ein in *handsal*. Just because I have found happiness in my marriage to Ein does not make me a man that flees females."

"I name you *warg*, Radulfr of Vejle, *outdweller* to this clan," Halldor shouted.

Radulfr heard Ein inhale sharply, but all he could do was stare at his *faðir* in shock. To be made a *warg* was to be branded an outlaw, someone that was the worst kind of criminal, no longer considered human.

Halldor was banishing Radulfr, making him an *outdweller*. An *outdweller* was someone who had committed a *warg* crime and become an outcast. They were made to live apart from the rest of humanity since by their action they had set themselves apart from normal humans.

"Very well." Radulfr kept his arm wrapped around Ein as he stood a little straighter and faced the man that had fathered him. "I will leave, but those that want to go with me will be allowed to do so. Fight me on this, old man, and you will have to fight me for my position."

"You have until dawn."

* * * *

Radulfr placed the last of his possessions in the wagon he had commandeered and turned to Ein. The man was looking sicker by the minute. The last week had been hard on Ein, changing his life in ways Radulfr knew Ein never expected.

Ein looked like he was ready to fall apart. He'd been twisting his hands together ever since they left the *langhus* after packing Radulfr's belongings. His face was pale, and every once in a while, Radulfr noticed a shiver running through Ein's body.

Radulfr would have preferred taking Ein somewhere quiet and loving on the man until he didn't have a single worry in his head. It just wasn't possible. They had too much to do and not enough time to do it.

Most of the villagers were alive. They had been rounded up and held in one of the large *byres*. After the battle with Fafnir, they had been freed to return to their homes or bury those that had died when Fafnir and his soldiers attacked again.

They had just a few more hours until dawn. All of Radulfr's possessions had been packed and loaded in the wagon. Vidarr and Haakon had also added their belongings as well as enough supplies to last several moons.

Radulfr just had a last couple of things to do before they could leave. He needed to talk to his clan, and he wanted to visit his *móðir's* grave one last time. He knew he would never be back. He needed to say goodbye.

"Come to me, *kisa*." Radulfr held out his hand.

Ein ran forward and grabbed Radulfr's hand, leaning into him. "I'm so sorry about all of this, Radulfr. I never meant for you to lose your clan."

"First of all, you didn't do this. Second, I would trade a hundred clans if it meant keeping you. You, little one, are much more important to me. I can live without my clan. I cannot live without you."

"Me either." Ein leaned closer and rubbed his cheek along Radulfr's clean shirt. "I just wish—"

"We'll build our own clan, *kisa*, one that accepts everything that we are." Radulfr chuckled and gestured to the men standing by the wagon. "Just look. We already have a few members."

Ein turned. Radulfr could feel the happiness filling his mate as they looked out over the small band that stood by them. Vidarr and Haakon supported Radulfr no matter what. They were more than friends. They were brothers-in-arms.

Baldr, Ulfr, Coinin, and Alimi had sworn their devotion to Radulfr as their *drighten*, even knowing what he was, or maybe it was because of what he was. Radulfr just knew deep down inside that they were true and faithful men, trusted men.

"More will join us, Ein, until we have the strongest clan wherever we decide to go."

Ein inhaled suddenly and swung around. His eyes were rounded. "I forgot to tell you. Njörðr told me where to go."

"Njörðr?" Radulfr swallowed hard. "Njörðr, the god of the sea and fertility and the *faðir* of Freyr and Freya? That Njörðr?"

Ein nodded. "My *grandfaðir*."

"And that would make your *faðir*…?"

"Freyr."

"Freyr, the god of fertility, weather, and phallic devices?" Radulfr swallowed and repeated his sentence structure from a moment ago. There just wasn't another way to ask. "That Freyr?"

Ein nodded again.

"By Thor's hammer." Radulfr closed his eyes and hugged Ein as close as he could get the man without being inside his skin. Freyr was one of the strongest gods in the nine worlds. He could be just as frightening as he could be benevolent.

"Radulfr, my *faðir* tried to take our baby from us, to keep him from being born."

"What?" Radulfr growled.

He might not be quite used to the idea that his little mate was carrying a child, but it was still his child, and he would fight to the death to protect both Ein and their baby. He'd even fight a god.

"Njörðr stopped him in time and sent him home but—"

"Why would he try to kill our child?" Some protective instinct made Radulfr reach down and cover Ein's abdomen with his hand. "He's an innocent."

"It had something to do with Freyr's infidelities and getting back in the good graces of his wife." Ein rolled his eyes. "I don't care what his reasons were. I never want to see him again."

"So, where is this place we are supposed to go?"

"Njörðr and Óðinn built us a stronghold, *Novgarðr,* along the Volga River. He said as long as we remain inside the walls, we will be safe. They have made *Novgarðr* a *frið-garðr,* a place of peace. Njörðr also said *Novgarðr* was large enough to house any that went with us."

Radulfr started to grin. His utmost concern was having a safe place for his mate and his child. Secondary to that was a safe place for those of his clan that wished to follow them. If this stronghold was as Ein said, Radulfr couldn't wait to reach it.

"We need to talk with my clan and see who of them wish to go with us." Radulfr started walking Ein toward their friends. "The wagon is packed, and we have a few more hours until dawn. We leave with the first rays of sun and not a minute later."

Ein nodded.

"I want you to stay with Vidarr and Haakon while I talk to my people. I need you to be somewhere safe."

"I am safest at your side."

"Ein, please, you—"

Ein cocked an eyebrow. "I am staying by your side. I am your mate. It's where I belong."

Radulfr could see from the firmness of Ein's jaw that the man would not change his mind. He sighed deeply and nodded his agreement. "Fine, but you will stay close to me at all times. Understood?"

"Understood."

"Vidarr, Haakon, I'd like you to gather everyone in the center of the village. Those who want to go with us need to be allowed to. Those who want to stay behind need to be warned of the danger. Jarl Dagr's soldiers will be here soon. They will need time to prepare for battle."

Vidarr and Haakon nodded and ran off to do as Radulfr bided. Radulfr turned to look at the four remaining men. "Njörðr and Óðinn provided us with a home to go to. I ask that you come with us but hold none of you to your oath of loyalty if you choose to stay."

Radulfr was not surprised when all four men knelt down in front of him and bowed their heads, baring the nape of their necks to him in a submissive gesture. He smiled and touched each one of them on the exposed skin.

When they stood again, he bowed his head to them, giving them his respect. "I thank you."

"We live to serve, *drighten*," all four men replied at the same time.

"For now, I'd appreciate it if two of you would take the wagon to the edge of the village along with our horses. We may need to make a quick getaway. I ask the others to stay here and keep Ein safe." Radulfr gave Ein a small smile. "The gods have blessed us yet again and given us a child. Ein must be protected at all costs."

There was a moment of stunned silence then loud wolf howls filled the night air. Radulfr grinned and tossed back his head, letting his howl join in with the others. It was a joyous sound, one of brotherhood and celebration. Even Ein got in on it, adding in his own human howl.

It was a moment of perfect harmony and filled Radulfr's soul to bursting. He just hoped it continued. He wanted this feeling of belonging to something bigger than himself. He just wanted the feeling of truly belonging, something most sought.

Chapter 13

Ein's heart ached as he watched Radulfr kneel beside his *móðir's* grave. Radulfr closed his eyes and bowed his head. Ein knew he was saying goodbye to his *móðir*. He wished he had gotten a chance to meet the woman. She had had a large influence on Radulfr.

Despite what Radulfr said, Ein knew the man's heartache was partly his fault. He couldn't feel bad about his mistake in mixing up the vials from Njörðr. He wanted the child too much. It was a symbol of all that was between him and Radulfr.

Ein walked over and stood behind Radulfr. He placed his hands on Radulfr's shoulders and closed his eyes. He had to bring Radulfr some measure of peace. The man worked so hard to care for others. It was time someone cared for him.

"Please, *grandfaðir*, help me ease his heart," Ein whispered silently up to the heavens. He wasn't really expecting an answer. The gods had already blessed them with so much. Asking for more was greedy, but he had to try. He had to do something to show Radulfr how much he was loved.

Ein's eyes snapped open when the wind suddenly started blowing through the small graveyard. He quickly looked around, expecting to see his *faðir* appear. Ein's eyes widened with fear and his hands tightened on Radulfr's shoulders when a ghostly figure appeared several feet on the other side of the gravestone Radulfr knelt before.

"Radulfr," Ein whispered.

Radulfr's head came up. He must have seen what Ein did because he suddenly jumped to his feet and pushed Ein closer to his back. The ghostly figure walked closer. At first, Ein could see right through it to the trees on the other side, but the closer it came, the more solid it grew until a beautiful woman stood before them.

"*Móðir?*" Radulfr whispered.

"Hello, my *sonr*," the apparition replied. "I have missed you."

"Ho—what?"

The woman smiled and gestured to Ein. "Your mate has brought me here."

"My ma—Ein?"

"Yes, he made a plea to the gods to ease your heart." The woman pressed her hands together and brought them to her lips. She looked giddy. "It was such a simple plea but was brought about by his pure love for you. The gods heard him and could not deny him."

"He loves me," Radulfr said simply.

"He does, and I could not ask for more for you. He will love you well until his dying breath, just as I have loved you. I can rest easy knowing he has your heart."

Ein peeked around Radulfr to get a better look at the woman that had given birth to his mate. She was beautiful, almost as beautiful as Radulfr was handsome. Ein could easily see the resemblance in their long black hair and deep azure blue eyes.

"Ein." The woman's eyes turned toward him. "Your *móðir* has told me so much about you. I'm happy to finally be meeting you in person."

Ein swallowed. "My *móðir?*"

The woman glanced over her shoulder. Ein's eyes widened as he looked past her to where another apparition was beginning to appear. He clutched Radulfr's shirt as the figure solidified and walked toward them.

"Is that... Is that..." Ein whispered.

"Ein, my beautiful little boy," the woman said as she drew up next to Radulfr's *móðir* and stopped. "My, how you have grown."

"Me?"

"Due to the nature of your mating and what you will mean to the nine worlds," Radulfr's mother said, "Eira and I have been granted permission to spend eternity together in *Valhöll,* watching over you."

Eira, Ein's *móðir*, stepped closer and held out her clenched hands. When she opened them, lying in each palm was a small golden bracelet. Each bracelet was simple in nature, braided gold entwined with small rune stones.

"Wear these," Eira said, "and wherever you go, wherever you are, we can find you and come to you in your time of need. Just call out our names and we will be there."

Ein's hand trembled as he took the bracelet Radulfr held out to him after taking both from Eira. He clasped it around Radulfr's wrist then held his arm out and let Radulfr clasp the other bracelet on his wrist.

He almost stepped back when Eira stepped up close to him. He didn't know his *móðir*. He didn't even remember her. He had been two days old when he had been forced from her arms and Jarl Dagr beat her to death.

"Oh, my *sonr,* our time together when you were born can be measured in moments, but I loved you a lifetime in those two days." Eira reached up and caressed the side of Ein's face. "I knew what would happen when Dagr discovered he was not your *faðir,* but I never regretted it. You are all a *móðir* could ask for in a *sonr.*"

"You knew Dagr would kill you?" Ein asked.

"I did, but it was worth it to bring you into the world." Eira's smile was filled with sadness. "I just wish we had had more time together before you were taken from me."

"I–I'm going to have a b–b–baby," Ein blurted out.

Eira's smile grew wider, happier. "I know. Óðinn told us, and we couldn't be happier about it. You and Radulfr will make a beautiful child together."

"When your time comes," Brynja, Radulfr's *móðir*, said as she stepped forward, "we have been granted permission to attend the birth of your child."

"And any other children you choose to have," Eira added.

"Other children?" Ein gulped. "What other children?"

The smile that crossed Brynja's lips worried Ein. The woman held out both of her hands, palm side up then leaned forward and gently blew across them. As her warm breath moved across her hands, an intricately carved box began to appear in her hands. It was made of silver, each side embossed with rune stones and designs. It was breathtaking.

"This is a gift from the gods," Brynja said.

Ein's eyebrows shot up. "Another one?"

Brynja chuckled. "This one is special."

"They all are," Ein protested.

Brynja nodded toward the box. "Ah, but this one will continue to bring you happiness for many years to come."

Ein shook his head and reached over to take Radulfr's hand. "Radulfr brings me happiness. He's all I need."

Brynja looked ready to burst as she opened the silver box and tipped the lid back. The inside was completely lined in white silky fabric. Right in the middle, in a small crevice in the bottom, laid a round glowing blue sapphire the size of Ein's fist.

An ornate design was carved into the top of the gem itself—two hearts entwined around a tree. Ein instantly recognized the tree as being the *Yggdrasill*, the world tree.

"What is it?" Ein asked.

"This is called a birthstone. Óðinn commissioned the dwarves of Niðavellir to find and shape the gem. Njörðr had the light elves of Álfheimr make the silver box, carving in the story of your lives," Brynja said. "They took special care when making it, Ein. They are your relatives."

"When not in use, the birthstone needs to stay inside this box and in a safe place. But when you decide to have another child," Eira said, "place the birthstone under your bed and the gods will grant you another baby."

Ein's jaw dropped open. He felt Radulfr squeeze his hand. "W–we c–can have more?"

"Many more, Ein. As many as you can love."

"There is one more thing, Ein," Eira said.

"More?" Ein tore his eyes away from the beautiful stone and glanced up at his *móðir*. How could there possibly be more? The gods had already given them so much. What would they want in return?

Eira reached into the silver box and carefully lifted the stone out. The gem glowed brighter the farther out of the box it came. Eira held it out in the palm of her hand.

"You will both live long and happy lives," Eira said. "That has been foreseen by the gods. If you accept this gift, your lives and those of your children will be forever entwined."

"We have a choice?"

Brynja chuckled. "In this you do. The gods will not force you to be together forever if that is not your wish."

"It is," Ein said quickly and without hesitation. "What do we need to do?"

"Radulfr, is this your wish also?"

"Yes. I would give up everything for Ein."

"Very well," Eira said as she turned the birthstone in her hand. "Bare your chest. The mark must go right over your heart."

"Mark?" Ein swallowed. "What mark?"

"The mark that will bind you and Radulfr together. It will bind your life threads together."

"Life threads?" Ein squeaked. He felt like he was pulling teeth trying to get information out of the two women. Obviously, they had spent a lot of time with his *grandfaðir*.

"Every soul has a life thread that ties them to the gods," Eira explained. "If you accept this mark, your life threads will be entwined, as will your souls. You will live together, but you will also die together."

Ein didn't even hesitate. He knew what he wanted. He reached up and started untying the laces that kept his shirt closed. "I don't want to live a moment longer than Radulfr."

Radulfr grabbed his hands, stilling them. "Are you sure, *kisa*? Our life is not an easy one. Many things can happen."

Ein smiled, feeling at peace for the first time since he had found Radulfr kneeling over his *móðir's* grave. "I've never been more sure of anything in my life."

Radulfr stared intently for a moment then the corners of his lips started to curve up. "If that is your wish, *kisa*."

Ein quickly finished untying the laces on his shirt, pulling the two edges apart. He could see Radulfr doing the same. Once both of their chests were bare, Ein turned back to the two women.

"What now?"

Eira held the stone against Ein's naked chest, right over his heart. Ein grunted, gritting his teeth as a hot searing pain burnt into his skin. The pain continued even after Eira removed the birthstone and pressed it against Radulfr's chest. Ein knew Radulfr felt the same pain when the man gritted his teeth and hissed.

But just as soon as the birthstone touched Radulfr's chest and he hissed, the pain began to recede. Ein frantically reached for Radulfr when his head began to spin. The moment their skin came into contact, Ein cried out.

He could feel their life thread entwining together, their souls becoming one. He could *feel* Radulfr—every thought, every feeling, every wish, and it was the most beautiful thing he had ever felt.

"Radulfr," Ein whispered. "I can feel you."

Tears sprang to his eyes at the love he could feel in Radulfr's heart. He had always hoped but he had never truly believed that

Radulfr would love him so much. But he did. Radulfr's entire soul was lit up with his love.

Radulfr smiled, a single tear falling down his tanned cheek. "Love you, *kisa*."

* * * *

Ein was riding high on the feelings coming from Radulfr. He was pretty sure he looked absolutely ridiculous with the big grin on his face and the bounce in his step. He just couldn't help it. Radulfr loved him, really loved him. Ein wanted to shout it to the worlds, all nine of them.

"Your happiness is contagious, *kisa*." Radulfr chuckled.

Ein beamed and bounced on his feet.

"We have one last thing to do and then we can get on the road to this stronghold the gods made us." Radulfr smiled down at Ein, grabbing his hand and kissing the back of it. "You seem excited, *kisa*."

"I think I am. We've been through so much in such a small amount of time. It will be nice to get settled somewhere." Ein wrapped both of his arms around Radulfr's thick muscular arm. "I'd like to have a safe place for us. I want to spend an entire week in bed with you."

"A whole week, *kisa*?" Radulfr smirked. "Do you need that much rest?"

"No." Ein grinned wickedly. "I need that much time exploring your naked body."

Radulfr's eyes rounded slightly. "I will see what I can arrange."

Before Ein could reply or make another suggestion, they walked to the edge of the center of the village and the noise level rose to an incredible level. Ein felt like covering his ears. Everyone seemed to be talking at once, and that was a lot of voices. Ein thought there must have been a couple of hundred people standing around the area.

Radulfr pulled him to the very center where a large platform was situated. When they climbed the steps leading up to the platform, Vidarr and Haakon joined them. Baldr, Ulfr, Alimi, and Coinin took up positions around the platform, one on each side. They had their arms crossed over their chests as if daring anyone to try and get past them.

Ein stayed back with Vidarr and Haakon as Radulfr stepped forward and raised his hands in the air. He clasped his hands together until they turned white. He wanted to appear composed. He felt like it was a losing battle.

Radulfr's entire clan stood before them, and they didn't seem happy. In fact, they looked like they wanted blood. Ein just hoped it wasn't his blood. The noise level continued to grow until Vidarr stepped forward and whistled loudly. An eerie silence fell over the crowd.

"My *faðir* has named me *warg*, an *outdweller*," Radulfr began, "because of the bride given to me in a peace-pledge with Jarl Dagr's clan is a man. I accepted that peace-pledge on good faith, and to break that oath would be to dishonor all that I am and all that I hold dear."

Ein tried to keep from cringing when Radulfr waved his hand back toward him. He could feel the weight of the crowd's stare as they all turned to look at him.

"Even if I could change the bride given to me in the peace-pledge, I would not. Ein has proven to be a fit and proper mate. I have no issue with him being a man and accept him as my betrothed."

The crowd began to grumble, but when no one actually said anything, Ein started to breathe a little easier. He turned to smile at Haakon when he heard someone in the crowd shout. A second later, something hit Ein in the forehead. He cried out and dropped the wooden platform, holding his hand against his head.

Radulfr roared as he ran over and gathered Ein in his arms, kneeling on the platform. He quickly checked Ein over. Ein winced when Radulfr probed the small cut. It was bleeding quite a lot, but head wounds did that. The cut wasn't actually that bad.

"Are you okay, Ein?" Radulfr asked.

"I want to go." Staying here didn't seem like much of an option. "Please?"

"Just give me a moment more, *kisa*, and then we'll go. I promise." Radulfr kissed the top of Ein's head then stood to his feet. He turned to Haakon. "Keep Ein safe."

Haakon nodded and took Ein, lowering his feet to the floor then plastered their bodies together. Vidarr came over and pressed himself to Ein's other side until Ein was sandwiched between the two men. A needle couldn't have gotten through.

"Ulfr," Radulfr said as he picked up a small stone off the floor and held it out to the man, "find the person that threw this rock and deal with them."

"Yes, *drighten*." Ulfr took off into the crowd.

Ein hoped Ulfr didn't kill whoever threw the rock. He wouldn't have minded seeing whoever it was get a good smack in the mouth, but he didn't want them dead. He was just sorry that someone felt like they had to throw the rock in the first place.

"Me and my men will be leaving this valley by dawn," Radulfr began again. "Those who want to accompany me, knowing full well that we will not be coming back, may do so. None will be penalized if they choose to stay."

The crowd grew restless. Ein cringed until he felt Vidarr's hand pat him in the middle of the back. It was a reassuring gesture, and Ein was thankful, but he didn't think he would feel better until they were on the road.

"There are two things you need to know before you decide. One, I have been gifted by the gods. I am a *Berserkr*."

The crowd cried out and moved back.

"My *faðir* seems to believe this is a *geas*. I do not agree."

"You are a *geas*!" Halldor shouted.

Radulfr ignored him and continued speaking. "You know me. You have lived under my rule for many winters. I have always done right by you. That will not change because I can become a *Berserkr*."

Halldor pushed himself to the front of the crowd and turned to look out over them. "He is a *geas*, a curse. He will bring the wrath of the gods down upon us. Even now, Jarl Dagr and his soldiers are on their way here to take vengeance for the death of his *sonr*." Halldor waved his hand back at Radulfr. "He killed Jarl Dagr's *sonr*. He has brought this down on us. He is a *geas*."

"Halldor is correct," Radulfr said. "Jarl Dagr and his soldiers should be here by dawn. I do not plan to wait around for them. The gods have provided us with a safe place to go. Those who choose to go with us are welcome. Those who wish to stay behind need to start preparing for Jarl Dagr's arrival."

"You would desert us?" someone in the crowd shouted. "Now?"

"I have been banished," Radulfr replied. "It is no longer up to me."

"We'll be slaughtered," cried another voice.

"You will need to confer with Halldor as to what you should do now. He's in charge now. My concern is to get those who wish to go with us to safety."

When Radulfr turned and held out a hand to him, Ein ran forward and took it. He curled into Radulfr's side, breathing in the man's strong masculine scent. It smelled like safety. It smelled like home.

"For those of you who choose to go with us, you have until an hour before dawn to gather your belongings and meet as at the southern road. Do not bring with you more than the essentials or any personal items you wish to keep. We will be traveling quickly and lightly."

"Is that it?" Ein asked as Radulfr led him off the platform.

"That's it."

"Do you think anyone will join us?"

"A few maybe, but the rest have been scared off by my *faðir's* claims. My clan is a superstitious lot. Even a hint of a curse being associated with my name will scare many away."

"I'm sorry, Radulfr."

"I'm not. If they are so easily scared, then they are not the people I thought they were." Radulfr shrugged. "Maybe this is a good thing. Halldor will find a way to make peace with Jarl Dagr, and this clan can live in peace."

Ein blinked in surprise as he watched Ulfr come out of the crowd and stalk over to the wagon. A smaller man was hurrying after him, a bag clutched in his arms. Ulfr grabbed the bag and tossed it into the wagon then grabbed the man and tossed him up on to a horse. He climbed up after him. The man was shaking, looking terrified, but he leaned back into Ulfr's arms.

Odd.

"Do you think they can learn to live in peace?" Ein asked.

"I can hope."

Chapter 14

Radulfr kept a close eye on Ein as they traveled. He had never spent that much time around anyone who was carrying a child. Beyond hoping they had a safe birth and healthy child and sharing a mug of mead with the new *faðir*, he never really thought about the process either.

Now, it was at the forefront in his mind. He worried that Ein was too hot or too cold. He worried that he wasn't eating enough or maybe eating something bad for him. He nearly lost his mind when Ein started throwing up every morning about a month after they left the valley.

He didn't know how expectant *faðirs* did it. It was nerve-racking. Vidarr and Haakon found it hilarious and teased him about it on a daily basis. When Ein wasn't getting sick or eating his weight in food, he was teasing, too.

After a while, Radulfr gave up trying to be strong and masculine and just gave in to the fact that he was on uncertain ground. He didn't have a clue what he was doing. All he could do was love Ein and keep a sharp eye on him.

That wasn't easy as he was responsible for a number of people. Of the three hundred members of the clan, only eighteen had decided to accompany them to their new home. Radulfr had hoped for more, but he understood that people were scared.

Some were afraid of leaving their homes. Others were afraid Radulfr might actually be under a *geas*. And still others disliked the fact that Ein was a man. Radulfr wasn't going to fight to change people's minds. He had other things to worry about—like getting everyone safely to their destination, wherever that was.

South for three full moons then east for two more to a stronghold along the Volga River did not exactly sound like expert directions. Radulfr just hoped that the stronghold promised wasn't a cave in the side of a mountain.

"Glad to be off that boat, *kisa*?" Radulfr asked as he rode up beside his mate.

Ein blanched. "I don't think I was meant to be a sailor."

"Nonsense." Radulfr chucked. "The *Vikingr* were made to be on the sea."

"Radulfr, I'm the half-breed *sonr* of the god of fertility, not *Vikingr*. Trees and gardens are more my thing."

"True, but you are also the *grandsonr* of the god of the sea. That means you should at least have your sea legs."

Ein laughed. "Try me when I'm not carrying."

Radulfr grinned. He reached over and snatched Ein off his horse and onto his own. Ein didn't even cry out. Radulfr knew he had to be used to it by now. He was snatching Ein off his horse to ride with him all of the time. He didn't like being separated from Ein.

"What are you doing?" Ein asked when Radulfr wrapped his long fur-lined cloak around the both of them. Radulfr didn't say anything, but Ein started laughing when he went for the ties on his pants. "Radulfr, we're not alone."

Ein was correct. They were not alone. Other men on horses followed behind them. They had given up on the wagon at a port city when they purchased passage on a boat. They could have traveled the entire distance by horseback but following a good portion of the trade rivers seemed a better choice.

Winter was coming, and Radulfr wanted to reach their destination before it set in. He didn't want Ein out in the cold any longer than he had to be. He also needed to figure out how to get everyone through the winter months without starving.

Radulfr sighed deeply and hugged Ein to him. All of a sudden, he needed contact with Ein more than he needed sex. He felt overwhelmed, and Ein eased him. So much could go wrong.

"What's wrong, Radulfr?" Ein asked as he glanced back.

"I'm worried, what else?"

Ein rolled his eyes. "You're always worried."

Radulfr grimaced. "I am, but I have reason to worry. I have a lot of lives depending on me, especially yours."

"We're going to be fine. I do not believe that the gods would send us someplace that wasn't safe for us. There's too much at stake."

"And that's another thing," Radulfr said. "If this child is so important, then why haven't we heard a word from anyone? The gods haven't told us if we're going in the right direction, what to expect when we get there, nothing. You would think that they would be keeping their eye on us."

"Who says they aren't?" Ein asked. "Just because we haven't heard from them doesn't mean they are not watching. But I believe they want us to make our own way, our own decisions. If they led us around by the nose then what would be the point of free will?"

"I suppose you are right." Radulfr ran his hand up and down Ein's arm, grounding himself with that small touch. "Winter will be upon us soon, and I worry that we will not be sufficiently prepared to survive. I can't let anything happen to you."

Ein rubbed his cheek back and forth against Radulfr. "Nothing is going to happen to me. And the gods would not send us into the wild unknown without some sort of plan. They want this to work just as much as we do."

"I hope you are right, *kisa*, for all of our sakes."

Ein smiled and wiggled around for a moment. Radulfr chuckled when he felt Ein's bare skin as the man pushed the edges of his pants aside. Ein grabbed Radulfr's hand and placed it against his hard cock.

"You should stop worrying and do something about this. It would be a shame to waste it."

"My mate is a wise man." Radulfr chuckled and wrapped his fingers around the hard shaft. He gloried in the soft cry that fell from Ein's lips as he began stroking him from tip to root. Ein in the throes of passion was a glorious thing to watch.

Radulfr snapped the reins on his horse to get them a little ahead of everyone else. As glorious as Ein was, Radulfr found he was jealous of anyone else seeing the man in such a state. Ein's passion was for his eyes only.

When they were several hundred feet in front of the others, Radulfr tied the reins together and let them hang down the horse's sides. He lifted Ein up and swung him around. He pulled Ein against his own chest then reached down to grab his ass with both hands.

"You, my sexy little *kisa*, have a beautiful ass."

"All yours," Ein panted, "only ever yours."

Radulfr growled, Ein's words striking something deep inside of him. He had taken Ein's virginity, and while it had been done in front of witnesses, he was the only one to ever experience the ecstasy of being balls-deep inside the man.

Radulfr grabbed the small bottle of oil he had taken to carrying on him and popped the top. He poured a small amount out into the palm of his hand and liberally coated his fingers. Once he was all slicked up, he replaced the stopper and put the bottle away.

He grabbed Ein's ass again and spread his cheeks. Ein moaned, and his head fell back on his shoulders. Radulfr stroked his finger over Ein's puckered hole, and Ein's cries grew louder—yet another reason he wanted to be in front of the group. Ein was not a quiet lover, a fact that drove Radulfr to distraction every single time the man opened his mouth.

"Do you like that, *kisa*?"

Every time Radulfr ran his finger across Ein's entrance, he pushed in a little until he could wiggle an entire finger into the tight hole. Ein groaned and pushed back. Radulfr smiled. His *kisa* loved to be played with, to be penetrated. He was the perfect mate.

"Gonna ride you hard today, *kisa*," Radulfr said as he slid another finger into Ein's ass. "Gonna ride you until you beg me to come."

"Now?" Ein's smoky gray-silver eyes were glazed over when he tilted his head up to look at Radulfr. "Take me now?"

"One more finger, *kisa*," Radulfr said. He would never take Ein until he was prepared, no matter how much he was aching. Radulfr brought his legs up a little and braced them against the side of the horse, lifting Ein's body up. "Get me ready, Ein."

Radulfr almost groaned when Ein's fumbling fingers brushed against his cock. He ached. He throbbed. He was about to explode just from those little touches. Radulfr could feel Ein untie his pants then pull the edges apart.

Just as Ein's fingers wrapped around his hard length, Radulfr sank a third finger into his lover's ass. Ein whimpered and started bouncing, impaling himself over and over again on Radulfr's fingers. At the same time, his hands stroked and caressed Radulfr, driving him to distraction.

"Time to turn around, *kisa*."

Ein cried out in protest when Radulfr pulled his fingers free. Radulfr understood his urgency. He felt it himself. He doubted he would make it more than a few seconds once he got his cock deep inside Ein's tight ass. The man was made to be fucked, and fucked often.

Radulfr had every intention of doing just that. He picked Ein up and swung him around until he faced forward once again. Radulfr pushed Ein down until he lay against the horse then lifted his ass up.

He couldn't help but pause for a moment when he spotted Ein's pink hole twinkling up at him. He rubbed his thumb over it, groaning when the little bud quivered as if begging to be filled.

"So perfect, *kisa*," he whispered in awe. He pushed his thumb in past the tight ring of muscles. Ein's ass seemed to suck him right in. "Look at how you take me."

Radulfr delighted in the full-body shiver that raced through Ein when he blew over the little hole. Ein was so damn responsive, too. Radulfr always knew if Ein was enjoying himself or not, either from word or body response. Ein hid nothing from him.

"Radulfr, please."

"Begging so soon, *kisa*?" Radulfr chuckled.

He knew how Ein felt. He was aching to be deep inside that quivering hole. Radulfr quickly transferred some of the lubing oil from his hand to his cock, getting himself nice and slicked up. Once he was ready to go, he pulled Ein back until the head of his cock rested against Ein's tight entrance.

"Take me, *kisa*. Take all of me."

Ein slowly moved back, sitting up as he did. Radulfr watched his cock sink into Ein's ass until Ein's body blocked his view. Once Ein rested back against him, Radulfr wrapped his arms around the man and grabbed his cock.

His hand was still slick and slid easily over Ein's engorged cock. Radulfr was so far inside of Ein's ass that his balls rested against Ein's. Radulfr used his other hand to grab them both, gently massaging them between his fingers.

Ein's body began to shudder. Hs head fell back against Radulfr's collarbone. His hands gripped Radulfr's arms until his nails dug in. These were all sure signs that Ein was close to erupting.

"Ready, *kisa*?" Radulfr whispered into Ein's ear. "I promised I was going to ride you hard so hang on."

Ein's cry filled the air as Radulfr nudged his horse into a small lope. It was exquisite. Every move the horse made caused Ein to bounce up and down on Radulfr, driving his cock in and out of Ein's ass at a fast pace.

"Faster!" Ein shouted.

Radulfr didn't know if Ein meant faster with the horse or faster with his hand, so he did both. He kicked the horse into a faster pace and increased the pace of his strokes. They hadn't gone more than a few yards when Ein screamed. Hot spunk shot out of his cock and splattered all over Radulfr's hand and the horse below them.

Ein's tight muscles clamped down on Radulfr's cock, adding yet another facet of being inside Ein. When the man came, he nearly always took Radulfr with him within seconds just from the pure ecstasy of feeling Ein come.

This time was no different. Within a moment of Ein coming, Radulfr roared and filled Ein's ass with his own release. Pleasure unlike anything he had ever felt with anyone else rocked through his body until spots swam before Radulfr's eyes.

He dropped his head forward and rested it against Ein's until he could breathe again. Ein was panting softly, little aftershocks shooting through him and right into Radulfr. Ein's inner muscles continued to spasm for some minutes, dragging Radulfr's orgasm out until he didn't think he had another drop of cum inside his body.

Once he could breathe and think again, Radulfr planted a series of soft kisses on the side of Ein's face. Ein turned and smiled, meeting his lips for a long kiss that topped off the sex they just had.

"Do you feel okay, *kisa*?" Radulfr asked when he finally pulled away.

"Hmm, I feel wonderful," Ein murmured, tucking his head under Radulfr's chin.

"Then you might want to get cleaned up and tucked away." Radulfr chuckled. "I can hear the others coming up behind us."

Radulfr burst out laughing when Ein started scrambling. He grabbed a cloth then pulled himself free from Ein's ass, groaning at the small quiver that surrounded his cock before he pulled all of the way free.

Radulfr quickly cleaned Ein up then himself. He tucked his cock back into his pants then helped Ein back into his. Once they were presentable again, Radulfr pulled Ein back against his chest. He grabbed the reins with one hand and pressed the other against Ein's abdomen.

"How is our little man?"

"Hungry." Ein laughed.

"You are always hungry."

Radulfr wasn't complaining. He liked knowing Ein was getting enough to eat. He reached into one of the bags hanging off the horse and pulled out some smoked meat pieces, handing them to Ein.

"Eat, *kisa*, and then you can close your eyes. I will hold you while you sleep."

It wasn't long before Radulfr had an armful of sleeping male. The others had caught up with them by then, Vidarr and Haakon giving him knowing grins. Radulfr just grinned. What else could he do? He held his world in his arms.

* * * *

"Wake up, Ein. I think we're almost there," Radulfr said softly as they rode out of the forest to a large meadow situated between them and the river.

They had to be close. They had been traveling for ages. Despite hoping that traveling by boat would cut off some of their travel time, it hadn't. They still traveled south for three full moons then east for two more. They had been riding along the Volga River for the last few days.

The countryside was barren of other people. They hadn't seen a single soul in days. The last village they traded at had been over a month ago. Radulfr had added more supplies then, since winter was drawing nearer.

Already, snow was starting to litter the landscape. The thick trees in the forest were dotted with white. Ice grew along the edges of the river. Snow-capped mountains could be seen off in the distance.

Radulfr wrapped the furs that covered them more tightly around Ein when the man opened his eyes and looked around. Ein rode with

Radulfr almost solely now that his pregnancy had advanced. Radulfr couldn't bear to be separated from Ein.

"We're there?"

"I think so," Radulfr replied. "I don't know what it is, but this place feels right. There's just something about the land that calls to me." Radulfr looked out over the landscape, impressed by the large dense forests edging along meadows of snow. "Can you feel it, *kisa*?"

"It's magical, Radulfr."

Radulfr rode a little farther, moving closer to the river across the slopped meadow. When he reached the top of the slope, he stopped and just stared.

"Ein, look."

Ein turned. Radulfr could feel the awe in his mate when the man trembled. He understood the shock. The gods had provided for them and on a grand scale.

A large stone bridge crossed the river. It connected the other side to the fields and trees on this side. But the other side was what held Radulfr's attention. The bridge led to a road that ran right up to a large gatehouse, huge turrets on either side.

High stone walls led off from each side of the gatehouse in both directions to surround what looked like an entire village. Radulfr could see hundreds of wooden roofs filling the inner walls. There was even smoke coming from many of them.

"Ein, this may be the wrong place. There are people here."

"No, it's not." Ein pointed. "Look."

Radulfr looked to where Ein was pointed. His jaw dropped open. He couldn't have uttered a sound if his life depended on it. A great fortress of stone had been carved into the side of a sheer cliff that looked like it reached right up into the sky.

The fortress sat above the village, a long winding road leading up to a second inner gatehouse. Another wall surrounded the area right in front of the stronghold, giving it a second line of defense.

"It's beautiful," Ein whispered. "Just like my *grandfaðir* promised."

Radulfr just nodded. The gods had created a place that would not only house them but hundreds of others. The inner and outer defensive walls would keep them safe as well as the fortress built into the side of the mountain.

Between the forest, the river, and the meadows, there would be plenty of food and trade goods for the coming years. Wildlife was abundant, wood for building and fires readily available. And the river would allow them a quick trade route with other villages.

That there were already people here was a bonus. Radulfr hoped it meant that the fortress was ready to be lived in as well as the village. With snow already on the ground, Radulfr didn't know how much more time they had to prepare for the colder climate.

Radulfr waited until the others had joined them then started his horse over the stone bridge. He wanted to see everything, to explore. He also wanted to get Ein inside where he would be warm and safe.

"Radulfr, look." Ein pointed to the stone over the outer gatehouse.

Radulfr felt yet another shock as he looked to where Ein indicated. Carved into the stone over the gatehouse was the word *Novgarð*. Ein was right. They had arrived at the stronghold built for them.

Radulfr kissed the top of Ein's head and pressed his hand over his large distended belly. Warmth flowed through him when he felt a small kick against his hand. Radulfr sighed, some of the tension from the last several moons easing away. He didn't know what the future would hold for them but it looked promising.

They had a safe place to live, a safe place for Ein to give birth to their child. Those who had come with them to this unknown land had become friends and comrades, men and women that Radulfr liked and trusted. And most importantly, they had each other. They had been truly gifted by the gods.

"We're home, *kisa*."

THE END

WWW.STORMYGLENN.COM

GLOSSARY

A
Æsir - term denoting a member of the principal groups of gods of the pantheon of Norse paganism. They include many of the major figures, such as Odin, Frigg, Thor, Baldr and Tyr.
Æsir–Vanir War - a war that occurred between the Æsir and the Vanir, two groups of gods.
Álfar - the Light Elves in Norse mythology that live in Álfheimr, "elf home".
Álfheimr - realm of the light elves.

B
Berserkr - Norse warriors who are reported in the Old Norse literature to have fought in a nearly uncontrollable, trance-like fury
Byre - barn that houses 80 - 100 farm animals

D
Demi-god - half god, half human
Drighten - warlord

F
Faðir - father
Fastnandi - the guardian responsible for Ein's interests during these negotiations
First bond bite - the first bite that bonds a Berserkr and his mate.
Freeman - these consisted of villagers, free servant to the drighten and his thanes, and merchants.
Freya - daughter of Njörðr and the goddess associated with love, beauty, fertility, gold, war, and death
Freyr - son of Njörðr, the god of fertility, weather, and phallic devices
Frið-garðr - an area of peace
Fuðflogi - man who flees the female sex organ

G
Geas - curse
Gerðr - wife of Freyr
Godi - singular temple priest
Godis - temple-priests
Grandfaðir - grandfather
Grandsonr - grandson
Griomenn - the homeman (house husband)

H
Hansal - a formal agreement of betrothal sealed by a hand-clasp
Heiman fylgia - paid by the bride's family to the husband.
Holmgang - a duel.
Hov - a spiritual commune
Huglausi - cowardly
Husbondi - master of the house

J
Jarl - the Scandinavian form of a title meaning "chieftain"

K
Kisa - kitten

L
Langhus - longhouse
Lawspeaker - speaker of the law like court judges

M
Meyla krafla mikli thur syr - "child born of a long dead sow"
Móðir - mother
Morgengifu - A second sum payable by the groom after the consummation of the wedding was also set at the negotiations
Mundr - the mundr was what most modern sources refer to as "bride-price.

N
Niðavellir - realm of the dwarves
Njörðr - (Njord) a god among the Vanir. Njörðr is father of the deities Freyr and Freyja, associated with sea, seafaring, wind, fishing, wealth, and crop fertility.
Novgarð - Novgorod is among the oldest cities of Russia, founded in the 9th or 10th century.

O
Óðinn - (Odin) a major god in Norse mythology and the ruler of Asgard
Outdweller - someone who has committed a warg crime and become an outcast

P
Peace-pledge - often the wife served as a "peace-pledge," bartered in marriage to guarantee the reconciliation between formerly feuding parties.

S
Sansorðinn - demonstrably sexually used by another man
Seið-kona - shaman or practitioner of magic
Sonr - son
Sorðinn - sexually used by a man

T
Thanes - warriors, similar to the medieval knights
Thing assembly - Every year, a general convocation would be held for the various tribes called the "Thing assembly"
Thingstead - where marriages were arranged or ratified, treaties were signed, disputes were settled, and criminals were punished

V
Valhöll - Valhalla, hall of the slain.
Vanaheimr- one of the Nine Worlds and home of the Vanir, a group of gods associated with fertility, wisdom, and the ability to see the

future.
Vanir - a group of gods associated with fertility, wisdom, and the ability to see the future. The Vanir are one of two groups of gods (the other being the Æsir) and are the namesake of the location Vanaheimr ("Home of the Vanir").
Vikingr - Viking

W

Warg - For worse crimes, such as oath-breaking, rape, treason, and willful murder, the criminal was no longer considered to be human. He was made a "warg"; meaning both wolf and outlaw, and became an outdweller.
Weregild - civil crimes. These were monies paid for wrongful or negligent death to the kindred of the victims by the perpetrators.
Wodan - means fury

Y

Yggdrasill - the world tree

ABOUT THE AUTHOR

Stormy believes the only thing sexier than a man in cowboy boots is two or three men in cowboy boots. She also believes in love at first sight, soul Mates, true love, and happy endings.

Stormy lives in the great Northwest region of the USA, with her gorgeous husband and soul Mate, six very active teenagers, two boxer/collie puppies, one old biddy cat, and one fish.

You can usually find her cuddled in bed with a book in her hand and a puppy in her lap, or on her laptop, creating the next sexy man for one of her stories. Stormy welcomes comments from readers. You can find her website at www.stormyglenn.com

Also by Stormy Glenn

Siren Classic ManLove: Blaecleah Brothers 1: *Cowboy Easy*
Siren Classic ManLove: Blaecleah Brothers 2: *Cowboy Keeper*
Siren Classic ManLove: Blaecleah Brothers 3: *Cowboy Way*
Siren Classic ManLove: Wolf Creek Pack 1: *Full Moon Mating*
Siren Classic ManLove: Wolf Creek Pack 2: *Just a Taste of Me*
Siren Classic ManLove: Wolf Creek Pack 3:
Tasty Treats, Volume 3: Man to Man
Siren Classic ManLove: Wolf Creek Pack 4: *Blood Prince*
Siren Classic ManLove: Wolf Creek Pack 5: *Love, Always, Promise*
Ménage Amour ManLove: Wolf Creek Pack 6:
Who's Afraid of the Big Bad Wolf?
Siren Classic ManLove: Wolf Creek Pack 7: *Pretty Baby*
Ménage Amour ManLove: Tri-Omega Mates 1: *Secret Desires*
Ménage Amour ManLove: Tri-Omega Mates 2: *Forbidden Desires*
Ménage Amour ManLove: Tri-Omega Mates 3: *Hidden Desires*
Ménage Amour ManLove: Tri-Omega Mates 4: *Stolen Desires*
Ménage Amour ManLove: Tri-Omega Mates 5: *Unspoken Desires*
Ménage Amour ManLove: Tri-Omega Mates 6: *A Hunter's Desires*

Ménage Amour: Lovers of Alpha Squad 1: *Mari's Men*
Siren Classic ManLove: Lovers of Alpha Squad 2: *The Doctor's Patience*
Siren Classic: Lovers of Alpha Squad 3: *Julia's Knight*
Ménage Amour ManLove: Lovers of Alpha Squad 4: *Three of a Kind*
Ménage Amour: Love's Legacy 1: *Cowboy Legacy*
Ménage Amour ManLove: Love's Legacy 2: *Cowboy Dreams*
Siren Classic ManLove: Sweet Perfection 1: *Sweet Treats*
Siren Classic ManLove: Sweet Perfection 2: *Mr. Wonderful*
Siren Classic ManLove: True Blood Mate 1: *Heart Song*
Ménage Amour ManLove: True Blood Mate 2: *Alpha Born*
Siren Classic ManLove: True Blood Mate 3: *Love Sexy*
Siren Classic ManLove: True Blood Mate 4: *Redemption*
Siren Classic ManLove: Katzman 1: *The Katzman's Mate*
Siren Classic ManLove: Katzman 2: *Dream Mate*
Siren Classic ManLove: Katzman 3: *Pride Mate*
Siren Classic ManLove: Midnight Matings: *Scales and a Tail*
Siren Classic ManLove: Midnight Matings: *Fang and Fur*
Siren Classic ManLove: Midnight Matings: *White Paws and a Dream*
Siren Classic ManLove: *My Lupine Lover*
Siren Classic ManLove: *The Master's Pet*
Siren Classic ManLove: *Fire Demon*
Siren Classic: *Wolf Queen*
Siren Classic: *His Gentle Touch*
Ménage Amour: *Mating Heat*
Siren Classic ManLove: *Shake, Rattle, and Roll*

Also by Stormy Glenn and Joyee Flynn

Ménage Amour ManLove: Delta Wolf 1: *Chameleon Wolf*
Ménage Amour ManLove: Delta Wolf 2: *Mating Games*
Ménage Amour ManLove: Delta Wolf 3: *Blood Lust*

Available at
BOOKSTRAND.COM

Siren Publishing, Inc.
www.SirenPublishing.com